Small breeze moves the curtains. In slow motion we undress. The breeze becomes a current, air turns wet, wind into water, miracle again! The river is over us and under us and I am on top of her, pushing down, pushing down with my pelvis, my breasts sweeping across her chest, and her hands locked into the skin on my back, and she is pushing up, with the same rhythm, the same breath, the same motion of fins gliding upstream. One wave, one rush, one which is us, the river everywhere, clear and fast, licking the pebbles of it, cold and fresh, our lips pressed together, our breasts joined like pyramids, their line in complete harmony, I push my stomach down into hers, which she is sucking in, and then she sighs her belly out, pushing mine in, springs creaking, turning over and she is on top of me, reaching down with her long fingers, rubbing the inside of my leg.

D1614309

Riverfinger Women

Elana Nachman/Dykewomon

The Naiad Press, Inc.
1992

Printed in the United States of America on acid-free paper
First Naiad Press Edition

Cover design by Pat Tong and Bonnie Liss
   (Phoenix Graphics)

Riverfinger Women was first published by Daughters, Inc. in
1974.

Library of Congress Cataloging-in-Publication Data

Nachman/Dykewomon, Elana.
   Riverfinger women / by Elana Nachman/Dykewomon.
      p.   cm.
   ISBN 1-56280-013-2
   I. Title.
PS3564.A27R5   1992
813'.54--dc20   91-38870
                                                          CIP

*I dedicate this novel to my grandmother,
who will never know now what went on
in her apartment when she wasn't there,
having been buried in the rain on
International Women's Day, 1973 –
because I always loved her,
and miss her terribly.*

A man is another person — a woman is yourself, caught
as you turn in panic, on her mouth you
kiss your own. If she is taken you cry that you
have been robbed of yourself. God laughs at me,
but his laughter is my love.

— Djuna Barnes

Lucy Bear and Rainbo Woman have disappeared. Therefore I, Inez Riverfingers, set down this, the pornographic novel of my life, with no regrets. The dough rises anyway, pierced as it is by arrows, and bleeding small bees that hover about the kitchen, searching for honey.

I have wondered what people who don't make love all the time do with their lives—and I have wondered this even though I have made love only six times this year, and was interrupted by the police one of those nights. They must have mistaken my abandoned sunday school, with its red urinal, for the abandoned birth control clinic down the block. Or, possibly, they were agents of the Committee (my friends tell me that's paranoia, and maybe it is, and maybe it's not).   (3)

They say it's sex that makes everyone crazy, and I believe it, though I am not quite sure how it happened.

End of Introduction. I am Inez Riverfingers, and I come complete with a vast family of the same. Some of their names: Ratatoville Riverfingers, Little Noodles Riverfingers, Natasha Riverfingers, Gabi-dog Riverfingers, Eulalee Riverfingers, Delphine Riverfingers, Holly Riverfingers, Bruce and San Fernando Blondie Riverfingers, Maggie and Al Bear Riverfingers, Peggy Warren (a closet Riverfinger), and Abigail, otherwise known as Abby Riverfingers (who chastizes me now, years after, in her letters from Jerusalem, for not taking another steady lover—god knows I've tried, but it's not an easy life for a dyke). Pickpockets, poets, acrobats, sociologists, tough street women, farmers and friends.

This list making reminds me of the Iliad. Homer squatting to take a shit on a hot day in the Aegean counting off the names, as his fingers rubbed the white rocks near the water-on-fire-beneath-its-blue-skin that he could not see, rambling on about many-horsed whomever.

"Who's that old fart, daddy?"

"Traveling storyseller son, one of that degenerate kind that go around buggering their own sex, relieving themselves on other people's lawns, blind to the beauty of the true cosmos, telling lies and getting drunk shamelessly on other men's hard-earned drachmas. Don't bother with him. On to the Agora."

(4)   °

Inez Riverfingers the first. Vital Statistics: 5'3", 160 lbs. approx., 22 years old, lesbian, fresh scar on left wrist, old scar over left eye, appendix scar, light scar on bottom chin from times it was knocked in ten-year-old rage on the pool edge, scar at base of throat from almost successful thirteen-year-old suicide, brown eyes, huge breasts, brown hair down to same, fair & smooth skinned, limps on left foot, small hands, bites nails, has never been known to mess with explosives, needs new boots and a dog of her own.

Living patiently in the abandoned sunday school. Stuck here to tell the stories. Of Abby who was her steady true love for over two years, starting ten days before they graduated from high school.

Of Peggy Warren who is friend to both of them and queen of the slightly seamy. Stuck here, at the end of another atypical early seventies college career, with only the memory, the smell of memory, of Rainbo Woman and Lucy Bear.

It's quiet in the abandoned sunday school, living with straight women, unformed women. Only the two-dimensional canvas comforts the hungry eye: young girls, summer, 1971; summer, '67; summer, '54; summer, '48; summer, '32—the young girls, the summer, the Scottish love songs, the young men getting their trousers sewn while the trousers are still on them, these years and the young girls sending boys away in the middle of the night, the hesitant one a.m. conversations:

"Well, what are you doing Monday night?"

"How should I know?"

"Well, I'm having a birthday party in the mountains, and I'd like it if you could come."

"Oh—oh, in that case, sure, if I can get back by Tuesday—I'm running off to join the circus, seriously, and learn trapeze, and I have to train on Tuesdays."

The young girls, their hair pulled back, their flannel nightgowns, their dogs, their kittens—their eventual marriages, their eventual children, their eventual returning and saying to the *odd person out:* "What happened to us? We did not mean to squander our world as we saw the world squandered. We did not really mean to give up so much of our young lives to raising children, to all the problems of having children, to reading Dr. Spock, making contracts with our husbands about the kitchen. We meant to live in the Eye of Art, live by

(5)

danger and by cunt cunning, by sharp pleasure and deep understanding—then how did we end up with these frog eyes with their filmy lids, tell us, tell us!"

I have not always been in these rooms, listening to and telling these stories. I have traveled in great arcs across the big cities of America and Europe, and the arches were always her legs.

For when she moved on top of me, sleepily, I thought: a giant ant lives inside her skin, ready to pop out any second devouring and I am frightened of her I cannot understand how it is, that we are all in such different bodies.

Girls in boarding schools, years with sadists, black leather jackets worn self-consciously, men picked up on Greyhound buses, one-night stands, Baltimore slums, New York and S.F. gay bars, hashish smuggling out of Tangiers, sisters and brothers in their underwear (looking at each other, listening to grandmother snore in the next room), funerals, acid and mescaline, the first promise of an armed women's nation, the coming together and the dropping away, days on the road, police in the night, taking over city hall in Oregon, planning the deals right, pimping on the side, code after code, a different language for everyone and everything—it is all true, and there are some who'd give large amounts for definite verification.

In a moment I will conjure Abby Riverfingers and Peggy Warren and the burden of inventing myself again will wear off, the story will begin. Peggy who is somewhere in Michigan or Minnesota, or was two weeks ago, making her way across to this coast; and Abby, one and one-half years dis-

tant, only letters in the space between San Fernando Valley and the Promised Land.

Moments have passed, and I will make Abby
reappear. It is as easy as this, a voice squeezed from
black plastic keys, telling stories in bed. The
hammering of myself into the background will
seem to be over. This hammering, this background
—the language of our getting older, the time of our
being no longer children but young women, that is
to say, forming into identifiable shapes, it is not
simple. From time to time you will hear that faint
tackety-tackety-tackety, like kids at summercamp,
making bronze name plates in relief dot by dot:

these are our lives, these are our lives, these are
our lives.

(7)

"Once upon a time there was a wonderful
bear, named Lucy. She lived in the deep magic
forest, on the other side of Talking River. What
made Lucy wonderful was not only how strong she
was, not only how beautiful—all gold and orange
colored in the early sun—but how kind she was,
gentle with all the other animals in that forest no
man has ever found. She never ate fish the way
bears in the world do, she would sing duets with
them instead as they swam along Talking River.
She helped the bees scout for good clover, and had
learned the secret bee dance, so she could tell them
where it was. The bees rewarded her by giving her
all the honey she needed, which she would eat

along with all the other wonderful berries that grew all year long. But there weren't many other animals her size in that place, so she grew lonely and restless. One day the River noticed that she was singing fewer and fewer duets, and peering farther and farther over the River's edge.

" 'What are you looking for, Lucy?' the River asked.

" 'I'm looking for someone big enough to dance with me,' she said. 'I'm thinking of crossing to find others more like myself.'

" 'Oh no, Lucy!' the River cried. 'There are dangerous men on the other side, who will capture you and dress you in ridiculous skirts and charge a price for your dancing and make you eat flesh, and keep you locked up for their own amusement—either that, or they'll shoot you outright.'

" 'But there must be another kind of people besides these men.'

(8)

" 'There is. There is another kind that walks, called women, but they're mostly afraid—afraid of each other and the men and of what the men tell them. Among them there are some who aren't afraid, who are trying to know something different, but they are outlaws and in hiding. One, called Rainbo Woman, is heading this way alone. Wait for her to come.'

" 'Okay,' said Lucy. So she waited, and began dancing the bee dance again, to pass the time.''

"Will she have to wait a long time, for Rainbo Woman to come?'' asked Inez, rubbing Abby's neck with her nose.

"I don't know yet. Stop that, it tickles, bum,'' Abby said.

"And when Rainbo Woman comes, will she turn Lucy Bear into a beautiful woman, will they live happily ever after?"

"Well, now, kid, I don't rightly know. You're getting ahead of the story. Maybe Lucy Bear will turn Rainbo Woman into Rainbo Bear, and they'll spend the rest of their nights growling at each other, their stomachs full of blueberries."

Abby turns to look at Inez in the Colorado street light, in their first apartment, a two-room converted attic. Peggy Warren sleeps in the other room, which is also the kitchen. Inez is curled on her side, cuddled into the hollow of Abby's thin arm, looking up. They fit. Seventeen, eighteen, thin to fat, not self-conscious, pleased to be there, seam against seam. Their hands trace each other, begin to touch as leaves touch in first summer winds. Unbelievable. All the forces of civilization had worked against this, still it happened. They *(9)* made love again that day, the last time before falling asleep. They had the freedom to touch while they were still children. No one had given them permission. They just made it all up, taking their freedom with their hands in front.

There was nothing in either of them that was older than seven, except that they knew how to do it, finally, after five weeks they had figured one hole from another. There were no movements putting pressure on their consciences, only safety in being two together. There was only the fairytale, being seventeen and sleeping in each other's arms in Colorado. These small protections they wove like nets, to keep away what they understood perfectly.

They understood perfectly about names and

rumors, psychiatrists and angry fathers, perverts, rotten ungrateful selfish vain children, disgust and fear, more fear, self-hatred, confusion, no women will let us babysit for their children if they find out.

They were beginning to learn to protect themselves by never touching or looking at each other in public. By waiting until they got into gas station restrooms when they wanted to kiss each other. By calling themselves roommates. By watching other people very carefully. By being children only together, in their first double-bed. Sometimes they were open with Peggy, who never told them until three years later that she was jealous, for wanting to join them.

Abby accepted it, because it was safe and at the same time exciting, a little dangerous—she knew it felt good, and she wanted it. She was very stubborn about what she wanted, when she was positive that she wanted it.

(10)

She had been stubborn with her parents for two years now about her independence. About not going to a Long Island suburban high school anymore after tenth grade. Her mother had screamed and cried, and her father had consoled her mother by sending Abby away to boarding school—first to an experimental school in the South which Abby had hated almost as much as the suburban one, and then to Highland Hills in Massachusetts, where she met Peggy and Inez. She was also stubborn with her parents about not taking any more money from them, except for school. She was stubborn to be on her own, to start really running, to build muscles at least eight ways. The plans for the octagonal cabin she was going to build in the wilderness were all drawn up, down to even which way the doors would slide. There would be room in her life to travel cross-country on horseback, and there would be room for horses to live inside her cabin in the cold mountain winters. She would take care of all the animals that would come to her, and she wouldn't bother with people.

Back on Long Island her family was saying: She'll grow out of it. It's a phase. So we spoiled her a little, because she was our youngest daughter, we let her be a tomboy, and she got a little willful. But she's young still, there's plenty of time for her to get married, like her sisters.

Whether or not they'd drag her back if they learned about Inez, about what was going on, was a question Abby was not about to risk answering.

She knew better than to trust almost anyone. She almost knew better than to trust Inez. What she saw *(11)* was that Inez was a little crazy. Many a woman has been a sucker for that one. Feeling protective. If only you would stop looking at your eyes reflected in windows, if only you would be happy, Inez, and ride horseback across country with me. We could take care of stray animals together.

Abby picked up worms so they wouldn't get run over in the middle of the street. She began to see Inez the same way she saw her cat, or the horses in her fantasies. To have that feeling about Inez, that she needed and would simply accept protection, returning simple sexual affection, was to come very close to trust.

Still Abby wasn't sure. What is this sex and living

together? What is going on here? She knew it wasn't wrong, it couldn't be wrong, to feel this. But what do the words mean anyway.

She knew that she would not let Inez hurt her, that no human being would get that close to her. She knew people wielded power over each other, seeing how her mother and father, good middle-class Jewish people, controlled each other with the power to make each other miserable. She saw all people trying to get that edge, parents over children, teachers over students, bosses over workers, lovers over lovers. She didn't understand why it was, but she knew she did not want it. She would go alone into the mountains first, with her camera, and be with the animals.

Inez heard Abby when she said, "I don't like people, I am better company for just myself, I'd rather be a hermit." But Inez knew that she could get Abby to follow her, just the same.

(12)

There are powers, there are ways, and Inez knew about them. Guiltily she extended a paw towards Abby, saying: I too am a creature, I am a wounded creature, nurture me. There was just enough attraction in their bodies and confusion in their heads to bind them.

A thousand fantasies multiply in that feeling—of marriages, weddings, houses hung with ribbons of safety. Abby was the first person who didn't hurt Inez—didn't make her feel freakish and clumsy. Inez knew what that meant, what the game was, how you had to hold on to it, opportunity only knocks once, she had read about it in books, she had read a lot of books, now it was her turn to play, to use her real body as a marker in the game. It would be good, it would be gentle, it would be so tender that they could make a movie, and get someone else to play her part (who wasn't quite so heavy). They could make a movie about Inez and Abby, so that people would see that lesbians are beautiful, there is nothing, nothing at all unnatural about them, they too can have weddings and be in the movies.

Some pornographic novel! Some novel! What's going on here anyway? Where's the sex, where's the action, the *angst*?

Let me try to make it clear. In 1967 we still wanted to repeat the same straight story. But we knew even then, in our careful duplications (toasters, laundry, feeding the cats, a whole inventory of living together), that we were pornographic because we were both women.

Nothing else—we were too modern already to believe that one of us was the man and the other was the woman. We felt like neither men nor women. We were females, we were queers ("but *I'm* not a lesbian," Abby said in Colorado, "I just love *you*, Inny."). We knew we had the right to love whomever we loved—it was part of the amorphous thought of a sexual revolution we found ourselves in the middle of. It was very democratic, theoretical, and very very personal. And we knew that when we made the movie about how good it was, how after all lesbians could live normal lives, have jobs, go to college, how they were the same, the same, really the same as straight people, only they were both women, but that was just—an accident—a matter of—chemistry—we knew that when men came to see the movie we would make, the men would come because it was pornographic, that's all, baby, sinful, immoral and certainly absurd, for women to think they could do it without them.

Let me try to make it clear. There is Inez. There is Abby. They became lovers when they were seventeen. This is the story of what it means to be women and lovers when you are seventeen, with the years just behind (moving them toward it), and the years just ahead, with everyone waiting to say, uh-huh, just as we thought!

There is Peggy Warren. She is smuggling hash from Tangiers, accumulating a thousand tatooed stories behind her eyes like veils that keep even her old friends away. She's been sleeping with every kind of man there is, sadists, baby pimps and North Pole engineers. She comes to speak about heroin and the (real) 42nd Street porno trade, massage parlors and organized crime. She is an old friend of Abby and Inez.

There are all the places where these stories touch each other and make the start of a common life, the beginning of an idea about community. There are all the places where the story falls apart and something else shows through—an isolation, a terror, a hunger to shape that isolation and terror into some kind of love for ourselves.

A hunger for each other, two hungers, three: one out of fear; one for metamorphosis (to be girls no longer, to be women, and serious); one for actual

(14)

love, whatever it is. There is a first powerfulness in knowing what our hungers are, that they may not be taken from us and be sold by Tampax or Pepsi-Cola.

When you're talking about someone's body, that's about as close as you can get. This is how it worked in our bodies, how our hungers worked into our bones. There was authority at every pressure point, trying to direct us (for our own good). We fought back with fads that nearly killed us. And slowly in our bodies words grew, formed a strength against both the fads and the pressures of our mentors.

We thought we were very special then, we thought we were hot shit, for being perfectly existentially unique, reading all the books by men about ultimate aloneness and the isolation of mass man.

We were exactly like millions and millions of others in the sixties and seventies and long before and after, self-important with big words like alienation and technological elite. It's the same story for every girl and boy adolescent who knuckled under waves of words they couldn't own: sexual revolution and hard rock and LSD. We were scraped along the sharp stones of those, where the undertow dragged us.

But in being faceless unmentionable nameless lesbians, unapproved by Ann Landers or Jerry Rubin, in being unable to find catch words in newspapers or the books we read in our dormitories, for that, for what that meant, women loving women—in that we could have no fads. That

(15)

was where some of us began our resistance, learned to change (acid on stone) who we thought we were doomed to be into who we are. Tough, strong, proud: free women.

❷ Highland Hills was no average New England boarding school. In your first week there you were ushered into the solemn chambers of the eighty-year-old foundress, Theodora Koenig, in groups of ten. She would say,

"Yah, now Karl he is dead these twenty years now. Yah, Karl is dead, but the meaning of his work, it is still living. Here at Highland Hills we vill not havf the free love, we vill not havf the marijuana. Many of you children think the free love is a good thing, but ve know better. Love is a good thing, and you vill love this school, I am sure of it. Sex, the sex, can be a good thing, but ve must understand it. Many times you children come to me and say, well, we are in love, so why should we not be having the sex? And I know that you havf these feelings, it is normal to havf them, but it will hurt you very much to be just doing the sex without knowing what love is. Karl had the idea that in our school, yah, we would learn to use this sexual energy of adolescents, yah, in ways that are good for them. To be putting this energy right away into the sex confuses everything. We havf a lot of work to do here at Highland, we think it is important for children to put their new energy into study and into learning how to make a school run vell. It is up to all of yóu now to run this school, yah. You must remember about the sex, and you must not smoke the marijuana. Many of you vill think I am just an old lady who doesn't know anything, but I know that it is very bad for you to smoke these things. Many doctors say so, and I see myself that the children here who do it, they do not any more love the school, yah, they do not anymore study, they are very confused then and we havf to let them go, yah. So."

Then Theodora would turn up her hearing aid and let you ask questions.

°

Inez came to Highland as a junior. She had been in a Quaker school in Maryland the year before, and had been thrown out for being a bad influence and a troublemaker. She had written editorials in the school newspaper wondering why the headmaster wasn't replaced and she was beginning to have dubious relationships with other girls. She had refused to go to modern dance one whole winter, on the grounds that it was unfair to offer only one winter sport for girls and several for boys. Highland was known for taking in problem children—one step away from reform school or mental institutions.

(17)

At Highland, things went differently for her. She began to visit Theodora in her apartments, they would read "the Faust" together, Theodora reading the German and Inez reading the English out loud. Inez learned that she could manipulate her history of suicide attempts and homelessness to get whatever she wanted. She was not sure exactly what she wanted at first, but she began to get ideas.

First she wanted the student newspaper, and they were glad to give it to her. They gave her a separate little building to run it in, a teahouse made out of marble with huge French windows that opened up on the hilly landscape. They gave her unlimited class cuts and never demanded that she turn over her amphetamine. They gave her the freedom to do what she wanted. Mostly, then, she did what she wanted fearfully, privately, just among the friends she was beginning to have, and away from school, on weekends with these friends in New York City.

Inez had one real enemy at Highland Hills. One that she chose as much as he chose her. Named Allen, and no Riverfinger. Both of them ran for Student Court that first year she was there (Abby and Peggy came the next one). Both of them stood up in the theatre, where assembly was, with its rows of blue and orange and red and green seats, and (18) denounced each other. Both of them won, and spent months arguing, though they never said they were enemies, ever.

Allen, you bastard, may you and your sister be telephone operators in hell, an eternity of blank plugs caressing your soft leathery fingertips!

o

Allen had this sister, Mary: the first time, that awkward horrible puberty, the first trial, the first girl, pretending to sleep on a huge, king-sized bed.

Mary had gone to the same Quaker school that Inez had been thrown out of. Inez knew that Mary had told—by the smugness in Allen everytime he looked at her.

Now think back to your own locker rooms in high

school: what a secret your breasts were, what a mystery your thighs were, how you looked at your body in the mirror and it was always so ugly (how did it get to be so ugly?)—your hips were too big and your breasts too small, or everything was too big or too small, and you had all this hair, you had a line of hair on your belly, and all the other girls knew you were ugly, and besides you didn't have a boyfriend, that proved you were ugly.

How much worse to know all the other girls looked at you and knew something was wrong with you because you were—a queer. You weren't a girl at all. You were a deformed being. They made lists of all the girls who were easy lays and all the girls who were queers.

At Highland it was prestigious to be an easy lay. It was the real women who did it (at sixteen), and didn't care. It meant you were cool and tough, and got what you wanted.

(19)

Think then what it would mean to be a queer. Hey, Lezzie, come over here.

o

Allen's sister, Mary: the first time, fifteen years old, just Inez and Mary, in a big kitchen, somewhere in Washington, D.C. Cutting chestnuts, nicking the linoleum (gold-flecked) with the little steel knives.

I can't remember what she looked like. She must have been dark, Allen was dark. I could make it up. I could say she wore little print blouses and shirtwaist dresses. That she didn't have many friends although she was not ugly or dumb. I do not know who she was. Her name was Mary. This tree has many rings, each year a depth, each shed layer of skin leaving its core within, its wound. She spoke to me in the kitchen:

"You know, Inez, I worry that maybe I'm not like other people."

"Why?"

"Well, I think—listen, you're the only person besides my psychiatrist who I ever talked to about this—"

"It's okay, Mary. I got a shrink too." Nick. Scrape. Little knife blade sends up a curl of plastic from the linoleum edge.

"I—I think—maybe—I'm—I'm cruel." Mary shrugs a little, looking downward, having admitted this.

"What?" I will tell you a secret about Inez Riverfingers—she has seen cruelty, as she was going to again (this conversation the leading up, a foreshadow of that strange man in his dark nightmare boots behind the sealed door of dreams), but she has no faith in it.

Some who stalk these pages will erect great temples to the act of puncture, the stab itself, but Inez reflects, ruminates on the sculptures that pain creates—that anyone should harm for joy (that is, not out of need, or fear, or being hurt first, but the dazzle of it) is a fact she can fathom, if at all, only by analogy.

"No, really," says our friendly catalyst, "I feel that somewhere in me there's a meanness—a—I don't know . . ." Mary proceeded to tell a story about dropping a cat from a second story window to see if it would land on its feet. It didn't.

"Mary, I think—you shouldn't worry so much

about it. I mean, we all—have feelings like that. My father told me on his knee, as a matter of fact, that people aren't really ever good or bad, they're just selfish. You know, for what it's worth, we're all nasty sometimes, right? But—*I* like you, and I don't think you're so mean, so I don't think you should worry about it, okay?" Okay, another great teenage sputtering.

Lying in the big bed, the king size, in Mary's (and Allen's) parents' bedroom, that night of Thanksgiving when we were fifteen and half asleep, Màry's body rolls over the imaginary line Inez had drawn down their sleep. Inez knows, but has never told. Inez told once, she was thirteen, she said to the psychiatrist, "I think I like women." And the psychiatrist said, "Of course, dear, but in a few years you'll like men. You shouldn't worry about it. A lot of girls come into this office and tell me they're homosexuals, and most of them aren't at all. I know you're not." Inez had not been sure up until that time what a homosexual was, but she understood from the psychiatrist's voice that it was a woman who liked women instead of men, and it was wrong. She also knew then that she was.

Now Mary's body rolls over the imaginary line in the huge bed (it is big, this bed, she must mean something, to come so close). Inez sidles a little closer too. Then their bodies are very near. Very near. God knows how long it takes, those small, jerky, D.C. movements, until their legs are together, toe to toe, then slowly exploring instep, and then a long hard rubbing of calf to calf, fast now, like that oh like that (is this it? is *this* sex? what is it? does she? am I? are we aware of this? is she asleep?

(21)

are we dreaming this?)—but bound up with a knot in the soft gut, terrorized by contact.

Black runaway Cadillac comes to a stop just an instant before the cliff, leaving its tire marks across the ledge. With a smell of burnt rubber (or was it sulphur?) Mary halts her leg and says to Inez:

"You got what *you* wanted, didn't you?"

Oh living oyster-locked November, have you no happy first seductions for your orphans to remember? Pilgrim with your muzzle full of suspicion and guilt, will you not reconsider and admit that desire *can* be tender?

Inez stares at her face in the bathroom mirror. Her fingers grab the washbasin rim for support and turn white with pressure: is that round-faced fifteen-year-old a freak, an invert who traps young girls in bed and steals their legs for illicit pleasure?

"Inez," Inez says to the mirror, heart thunking. "You monster, you queer!" First the Pilgrim shoots the turkey, then he shoots the Indian. Inez sits up on the bed edge all night, watching car lights through the bay window, smoking Camels.

"Daddy, daddy," she says, to the man in her mind, who is saying *no*. "Daddy, I didn't mean to, I didn't mean it." Then the girl leans her head against the cold glass and weeps. The buckshot of shame is everywhere, there is turkey blood on the snow.

Peggy? Are you out there? Where are you? How will I find you? I'm tired of waiting here, while the hash sells. High school was such a nightmare—the taste of chalk and dust, the iron breasts of parking meters in New York City—the Riverfinger family wandering in the night, so many separate beds, so many stories.

All of us trying so hard to be respectable at seventeen. Members of Student Court and Student Council, at least yearbook photographers, earnestly attacking the issues of high school: dope and drinking and sex in the basement and who kicks out whom for what infraction of which rules, and who ranks.

I remember when I first saw you hanging onto Allen's arm, walking into the dining room. What a cool little bitch I thought you were. So blond and so straight and so hanging onto Allen's arm. A lot of nerves jumped along the lines of our sexual allegiances in high school. It took at least a certain amount of guts to get into the game.   (23)

We take you back, Peggy, you cunt, to the summer between my junior and senior year: to the apartment of an whole host of gone Riverfingers— Holly, my best friend from my junior year, who had graduated before me and was living in Greenwich Village with Greg and Neil (gay boys Holly had known for a long time) and Celeste, who was my roommate before Highland gave me a single. Allen came to visit Holly there, and his visit hurt me in front of my friends, Peggy. I was new to having friends, and it was intolerable to let them see me be hurt by him. It didn't help much that he was your boyfriend, it didn't help the tension between us at all.

o

Summer, '66. Bleecker Street, one-room-and-a-large-closet flat, Greenwich Village. Somehow two quiet cabinet makers, Greg and Neil, had been singled out to watch a generation of Highland kids march through their privacy, kick their cat (Sappho), sleep on their floor, drop acid, tune in Alfred Hitchcock reruns on the telly, use up what small amount of toilet paper there might be, all because Greg had dunked Holly's pigtails into little-red-schoolhouse inkwells in Vermont some prehistoric time ago.

Holly was twenty then, too old to be in high school, lived in the dorm room next to me, weighed 190 pounds and had tiny, pimple-like breasts anyway, and puffy eyes impossible to open in the morning, having usually spent the night before drinking herself to sleep.

(24)

("Arise, arise my friends, the morn with its rosy fingers, the dawn with its chill, the light that chases the night downhill howling, has come, it's time for breakfast."

"Dammit, Inez, close the fucking shutters."

"Holly, wake up, please, *please*—we'll all be late again to breakfast."

"What the hell do I care? Harold'll excuse me."

"Not again. I'll be back in ten minutes. Now try hard and get up.")

Holly was a great, expansive, brilliant young drunk, much like her mother, who was a great, expansive, not so brilliant old drunk, the only parent among us at Highland to have earned any nickname at all (The Bawd, we called her, when she would come to visit Holly and take us all out to dinner). Before Holly graduated that year, she had gotten into the habit of going to New York nearly every weekend to stay at Greg and Neil's. Celeste (who was my roommate) and I got into the habit of going down with her. It beat birdwatching in the Berkshires hands down.

Kind woodworkers, Greg and Neil, their precarious hole-in-the-Village becoming an excuse for atmosphere and experience to hungry Highland weekenders, who bathed Celeste with perfect gentleness one night when she was crawling around naked screaming:

"I'm Lady Godiva, goddammit, Holly, get me my horse! Inez, don't just stand there, salute me when I ride by." Inez was impressed. She had seen Celeste dress and undress all year but to see her exult in her good strong body, her nipples erect and sweeping into the slum dust, was amazing. Almost as amazing as it would have been if Celeste had turned to Inez one of those long dormitory nights and said: Why don't we sleep together tonight (as Inez fantasized every time they turned out the lights).

"Oh, you're too too gentle!" Celeste gigled, to good Greg, who picked her up, impassive, and ran the bath with her lying there in the cold enamel, and soaped, impassive, her birth marks and pimples, her armpits and butt-dimples, with the help of Neil and Holly, and put Celeste to bed.

Holly watched Inez looking at Celeste and saw the fantasy gathering up in Inez, who was too frightened, even knowing Celeste was drunk and wouldn't remember in the morning, to touch her then as the others were doing.

Holly was twenty, she was in love with Greg even

knowing that Greg loved skinny Neil. Holly was older and was beyond the bickering and the first fear that is our sexuality coming. She would hand Inez another beer then, and say, "Don't worry about it, kid," and Inez was never sure right then, during the school year, if Holly understood what was going on in her, how she would drink four beers, go out into the streets and walk around glowering at the tourists saying "Celeste, Celeste, Celeste, Celeste, Celeste, Celeste, Celeste," under her breath.

Holly herself wasn't having such a hot time either. Every weekend when she saw that Greg was going to sleep with Neil and not her, she would find some middle-aged insurance salesman in a bar on Avenue A and wake up in his bed not knowing where she was until she would finally remember Celeste and Lady Godiva and Inez and Greg and Bleecker St. and the five forty-five Greyhound bus they *had* to catch back to Highland where these sad, grizzly evenings were made over into romances, into legends of the big city.

The big city and the high school girls: an interjection into the story Inez is trying to tell Peggy about how Allen hurt Inez in front of Holly and Celeste and Greg and Neil; the story Inez is trying to tell Peggy about what it was like for Inez in high school, so that Peggy will know how inevitable it was, after all, that they should start out this friendship, this partnership they have now, as real enemies:

Virginity.

Has it always been a burden in just this way? The

way being: how will I get rid of it? To whom shall I give it, when? Must I do this just to prove I'm not frigid, so that I can reclaim the right to say: "No, I don't want to" which I don't have, because all the boys know I'm still a virgin? How will I know when I am no longer?

Here: I put my fingers between the lips and I rub down: so—first there is that bump (what is it? does the piss come from there?) no—the piss comes from this next little hole right above the big one—is the virginity there? Have I broken it by using Tampax? How can it be a pleasurable thing, to lose it, to break it? If it breaks, like magic, even if I cannot find it with my fingers, will it hurt? Will I lose a lot of blood (that girl, in Sylvia Plath's book—can it really be that bad?)? Shouldn't I find someone I care about very much before I do it? How will I know how? What is *it*? What does it feel like? Will I be different without it?   (27)

All of us made a vow to lose it by the time we were sixteen—or eighteen, anyway, at the latest. It has little to do with men at all. It is a ritual, and it is performed for our own benefit.

One girl turns to another in a room and says "I want to be pregnant" and it has nothing to do with men. It is a stroking narcissism of the sensual belly (still afraid to masturbate directly), the original solipsism, a way of saying "I want to be, I want to be admitted to the world, I want to mother a child if that is the only way to be a child no longer." Over and over in bathroom stalls during study halls, one friend whispered to another: "I lost my virginity last night"—and suddenly it's a badge of pride, that piercing, and a taunt to the girl who is still a virgin: "You are not grown up yet, you haven't made it, you're not free."

Battleground not of persons but of t.v., the movies and True Romance comic books, that sweet, hoarded commercial product, electric female genital apparatus! There is a fear of retribution, of good girls don't and a family in disgrace and this road leads to the gutter and what will happen if I need an abortion?

But it is done anyway, usually with a boy one knows casually (whose own private, desperate account is first marked *paid* and filed with the guardians of passage into coming of age), or has been going with; done usually with a lie still wet on the lips (the lies about the feeling they have for each other). Then each is free to make deeper involvements, to dredge and dive in the mystery of their own specific sexuality, of the specialness in whom they choose singularly to bed.

(28)

Those of you out there saying, "Come on now, what do *you* know, Inez Riverfingers? You yourself said you were a queer, where did you learn all this?" can be quiet now. I sit here, on this platform, when I should be asleep, reinventing life, and I know that I'm a woman. I too had to run this gauntlet, I too thought I would never get through with it, I too lay awake at night, thinking and thinking about it. Definitely, quite definitely, I am a woman—and have wanted to penetrate all the myths of that woman. The Mystery Woman, the Fair Woman Who Lives in the Country (Queen of Wands), Woman on Horseback, Woman of the Dunes . . . young girls in the summer, at school, dancing, swimming, drinking cider, crying, wondering what does it mean, this: to have a square centimeter in between the legs that's been so glorified we *have* to get rid of it to be ourselves. And what about these breasts, these wombs, this blood? I have lain awake thinking and thinking about it, I have thought about it in every ounce and muscle of my body.

"*Some* women," Holly said to Inez one night, when she had conned a Village cabdriver into buying her a bottle of gin. "Some women are *never* virgins, take it from me, Inez, and don't worry about it, *there's nothing to lose.*" She winked. She drank gin from a paper cup. Being on Student Court, Inez wasn't supposed to know about the gin. Holly winked. "You just do it, kid. It's not something to think about very much."

°

Back to Bleecker Street, summer '66. Our cast of a thousand virgins narrows down to six kids: Inez, Holly and Allen—Greg and Neil and Celeste watching in the background. (Remember Allen? Doomed to be a telephone operator on the Beelzebub exchange?)

Holly had moved in with Greg and Neil (who still hardly spoke, just watched the coming and going of the Highland troops) after graduating. It was August and everyone was on the road. It was hot and we drank a lot of beer. Inez had been crashing there, on the floor, for three nights. Celeste was running away from her first husband for the first time. Greg and Neil had built themselves a bunk in the closet (innocent of all metaphor), where at least they could close the door. Holly slept with whomever it was that she wanted, on the one mattress, and there was a rug laid out next to the mattress for such as Inez. Holly had tactfully persuaded Celeste that it wouldn't be a good idea for her to curl up on the rug next to Inny. Celeste understood by then anyway. She was staying with a friend of Holly's down the block, though she came over in the afternoons to get drunk with us and roll joints.

It was August and everyone Inez knew then (that is, all the people pressed into the tiny apartment) knew that she was not about to get into men. They knew it with discretion, and she knew that they knew, and that they were friends. Except for an occasional helpful teacher, Inez was not much pressed to prove the point, though whether it was out of cool or the general paranoia about discussing homosex, masquerading as cool, Inez was never sure.

(30)   It was August and hot on Bleecker Street, as I've said. We were drinking beer. At sixteen I had a hard time developing the knack of it, but it was parcel to the image (city woman) and I drank as much as I could. Smoked Camels then, too. Downstairs the buzzer is pressed and Neil gets it quickly.

There is one window in this apartment, which faces into a blind courtyard. The apartment is green and peeling. Its main decoration is a plaster imitation of a Roman nude—with a huge penis made out of silly putty stuck on it (SWAK engraved on its tip), pink and shiny: a birthday present from Neil to Greg.

At one end of the apartment, near the door, is a sink, stove and refrigerator combination. The refrigerator has half a bottle of red Gallo wine and three onions in it. The stove is covered with grease, two layers of frying pans deep. The bathroom is down the hall, there's hardly ever toilet paper, it has no windows, you have to pull a chain to flush it, and the chain does not always work, ditto lightbulb. Four apartments on the floor have the key to this bathroom. The rent, in 1966, is $80 a month. I tell you all this not because I am interested in social conditions in American subcultures, but as a simple student of the descriptive narrative.

Neil returned after answering the buzzer three paragraphs ago to let Allen climb the four flights of stairs and come in—Mary's brother, my fellow Student Court member, Peggy Warren's boyfriend-to-be.

"Hiya Holly, howza girl? Hiya Inez, long time no see."

On like that. There are all these bodies in one room now, and the beers are sixteen ounces. I had finished three and knew that somewhere after the fourth or fifth I would be sick for sure (and have to puke in the greasy sink, unable to find the bathroom key). Allen kept talking. I had never heard him talk so much.

At one time he had tried to sleep with Holly— although Holly was in no sense of the word a goodlooking chick, she was not ugly, and she was older, and knew something about the world (i.e., fucking). (Allen never got that far.) Allen was flushed and nervous. Holly was bored. Celeste had talked Neil into giving her a backrub by convincing him it would be good for the muscles in his hands. Greg was biting his nails. I was getting scared.

"Well, wadya think this next year will be like, Inez?"

"I don't know." Slurp. Slup. Allen and me were the only two in this collection fated to go back to Highland.

"Whataryou doin' before school starts?" he asked.

"I'm going to Washington—"

"Gonna see my sister?"

"I don't know—maybe."

Allen pauses. He begins to smile. This crooked smile smears itself on his face. "You know," he says, holding the beer can between his legs, "my mother—she was talking to the mother of a friend of yours down there—yeah, Donna's mother, I think, and my mother told Donna's mother that you're ah—you know—a lezzie. She said that's why you got kicked out of that school Mary goes to. Hahah ha hah hah ah—wadya think of that? She said Donna's mother isn't going to let you hang out with Donna anymore, if you go down there—boy— I couldn't believe it—hahahahaha—whadya think of that, Inny?"

"Hahahahahahaha," I said. "That's pretty funny." Neil has long since stopped rubbing Celeste's back. Holly is turning a little green. Greg turns around and starts fumbling with the stereo set that hasn't worked in three years. I am picturing Inez Riverfingers tarred and feathered in the nation's capital, friendless again.

"Yeah," Allen goes on. "Yeah, I thought it was pretty funny. Inez? I said to my mom, you gotta be kidding—she doesn't get into men *or* women, do you, Inez?" Now Allen is looking at me very carefully. For a while I look like the most important thing in the world is the beer I'm drinking, but then it's empty. I have no idea what to say.

Maybe you do not understand this after all. This whole episode. Spears of longing plunged between the ribs, with barbed heads. Can you imagine what it is like to be sixteen years old just once in your life? Do you know what it's like to know that your sexuality is at best a joke, three flights up in Greenwich Village, at worst, a weapon that people will use to sever you from them forever, to keep you from making friends with *their* children?

"No, I said to my mom, you gotta be kidding. Inez couldn't be like *that*—right? Boy, I don't know, Inez, but, you know how mothers are, they get all these ideas in their heads. Hahahahhaha." Allen's smile widens and his eyes sharpen. No one else is laughing. Celeste has sat up, and is exchanging meaningful looks with Holly, trying to get (33) Holly to do something. Allen keeps giving Inez this large wet grin. Then the time has passed when a snappy reply could have gotten me out of it, could have turned the burden of what this fool was saying on to him. In 1966 we never thought of kicking people like Allen in the balls. And he had won, something, some power, by knowing that his mother was telling the truth. That Inez Riverfingers was a queer. And Inez knew that he knew.

"Hey, Inez," Holly finally says, "we're all out of beer, dammit. I'm gonna go get some more, wanna come?"

"Yeah, okay. Catch you later, Allen."

We are down on the street now and I am very quiet. I am ashamed and I am very alone.

"That bastard, Allen," Holly says, as we cross the street to the liquor store. "Listen, baby, you don't have to take that kind of crap, I'm really sorry I let him even begin . . . two packs of Budweiser please . . ." We come out of the store and Holly puts her arm around me and I know she is pretty drunk but I think that Inez Riverfingers has never been so grateful in her life for an act of friendship. "The older I get," Holly continues, "the more I feel that affection in any form—in *any* form—is the only good thing there is in this shitty world. You got that, kid? Listen, Inez, I don't want you to let that deadhead bother you, because you're okay, you know?"

"Do you think I should still go to Washington to see my friends?"

"Goddammit, of course. I think Allen made that whole story up to see what you would do. Maybe not, he's not that smart . . . I don't know and I don't give a shit. Go to Washington and forget about it. He's not worth it."

"Okay. Holly?"

"Yeah?"

"Thanks. I mean really."

"It's nothing, baby, we gotta stick together."

(Whores and dykes of the world, unite.)

"Yeah."

o

When Peggy Warren started going with Allen, in the beginning of Inez's senior year, there was nothing in the cosmos that could have persuaded Inez Riverfingers to trust Peggy Warren for a minute. A conversation ran between them, though they never stopped to say it out loud, it was just sneaky whispers, Peggy spreading gossip and Inez panning in her newspaper every role that Peggy played in the school theater. The hidden conversation went:

"Tight-assed WASP"

"Fat slob kike"

"Think you're some hot actress"

"Think you're a writer, with your didly-shit newspaper"

"Machiavellian Student Council bitch"

"Megalomaniac boot-licker hypocrite"

"Cunt"

"Queer"

Remember that, Peggy? Hey, Peggy, you out there? Drowning in road maps of Los Angeles, trying to find me? Hey, Peggy, before I come back to the present, before I go to sleep tonight, before I write about how it was between you and me, and you and Abby, and Abby and me, I would just like to say goodbye to these other friends of mine, that I never got a chance to say goodbye to, whom I hardly even think about, anymore. (35)

Goodbye Holly. Did you really marry that black guy and move to some little town in the state of Washington? I've tried to find you in Washington, but none of your names are ever in the directories of the towns I pass through. The last time I saw Neil, about a year ago, just after Greg had left him and moved back to Vermont, to plant his own and grow his own and build his own and be alone, Neil said:

"You know what Holly did? I still can't believe

it." As you might expect, his voice is a little high, his eyebrows a bit satanic (but why would you expect that? Suppose it is true, that his voice is high, as men's voices go, that his eyebrows arch—what does that mean? Suppose he had the body of a quarterback, and his voice was high and his eyebrows arched? Neil was a young man that I was afraid of myself, fearing that he didn't like me, knowing he didn't like women.

"I still can't believe it," Neil said, "Holly wrote Greg and said she wanted to come back and be with him very much, but she couldn't right then, she had so many . . . debts. Well, Greg wrote her back that he wanted her to come very much, if she'd tell him how much it was. She did. It was about four hundred dollars with the airfare—and *that* was the last we ever heard of Holly."

I laughed. It seemed like the last panel of a Sunday comic strip. I was beginning not to take these people seriously. I was not sure why, except it was coming up in me, a sarcasm and belittling, which had a lot to do with learning not to trust. The old slow inside lesson of number one first.

Neil didn't notice it. "What *worries* me about it is—Holly would always come on like that's the kind of woman she was—but for her to actually *do* something like that—and to Greg!—well, she must think very badly about herself if she's that desperate. And she must be pretty desperate."

"Goodbye, Neil, thanks for the joint."

"Sure, Inez, thanks for coming by. You know what they say—old friends the best."

"Old friends the best, Neil."

"Goodbye."

(36)

Goodbye Bleecker Street. Everyone is moving uptown, or out to the country, or else to Christopher Street. I wonder only if you are still alive out here, somewhere on the Coast. Dark Riverfingers, dank Riverfingers, falling stars hopping around the sky like Mexican jumping beans in the Riverfinger night: thank you, Holly, forgive me the mornings I felt it my official sixteen-year-old duty not to let you sleep, thank you, goodbye.

What the fantasy was for Inez Riverfingers as a Junior
    or
Why they gave me a single room when I was a Senior   (37)

Inez Riverfingers watches Celeste sleeping. Five a.m., the seams of the night splitting. She imagines Celeste sitting on her bed one day, looking Inez straight in the eyes, smiling. Celeste's hand goes down under the blanket, starting in slowly on that smooth expanse of stomach between belly button and breast.

"Like this?"

"Oh, Celeste, you don't know how many times I have done this to myself, thinking that my hand was your hand, my breasts were your breasts and I was finally touching them, finally, Celeste—"

Alone at five a.m., index finger wrapped in the lips of her own vagina, Inez had an image of

Celeste's dissatisfaction with men: how Celeste would wake first, in the morning, beside her spilled-out teenage lover, his prick all limp and lumpy, and that awful smell of come on the sheets, and his hair greasy, his jaw droopy and snoring, how Celeste would wake first, and find no kindness in the larded sheets.

Ah, Celeste, Inez says, to her sleeping roommate: I would never let you down, I would never hold you *only* for the sake of pleasure—you'd sleep in the crook of my arm, your blond hair would lie along my shoulder, reeds at a pond edge, your nose, your cheek would cuddle where now only my hand cups my breast—when you woke, I would be awake too, always, we would smile and caress with the sun just up, coming through the curtains, Celeste.

"No, that is not it at all, that's not it, at all." T.S. Eliot

(38)   "I am looped in the loops of her hair." W.B. Yeats

". . . . ." Bob Dylan

A whole head full of men's literature and lyrics. Where were the New Haven and Chicago Women's Liberation Rock Bands when I needed them?

Celeste is part of the design in the background— another name from the years when it seemed I would always have two lives—growing farther and farther apart, one where I went about the business of living, and the other where I dreamed that someone would love me.

I want to invent a chapter where Celeste enters, saying: "Inez, I see something now that I didn't see then. Affection is holy. Your love for me was holy.

These distinctions that kept us apart are a farce. I am unlocked. I want to make love with you, to share love with you."

"About time," I would say. "You do not know how many nights I wandered freezing streets muttering your name, searching for your face. My love changes as I change, Proteus, slippery midwife of the sea, at one instant the egret that watches fish flash in stream with an eye all set to dive in the clouded hot sky—and the next, the fish, a sense beyond senses telling it to disguise itself as a fern. But however I change shape, the love once loved always always stays."

We'd cross the back of our hands between our faces for a sign, our faces would draw close through that double-sided frame—we would kiss, for the first time. Existential isolation is dead!

Celeste?

(39)

Peggy Warren: 5'2", 98 lbs., naturally blond hair, well-proportioned, creases around corners of mouth, habitual tea drinker, occasional affected English accent, speedreads detective novels and French literature, theater major, has no visible scars. Sixteen in this chapter, a junior at Highland Hills Co-Ed College Prep High School, arriving with a suitcase full of sexual wounds (among the fourteen boys she'd slept with a sadist who kept her locked up nearly a year in Scarsdale). A direct descendant of a Mayflower stowaway, qualifying her for membership in the D.A.R., Peggy Warren is the only woman I have ever met who'll die before I do.

Abby Riverfingers will last forever: 5'3" without her hiking boots, 110 pounds (all muscle at seventeen), blondish-brown long hair hiding the soft lines of her face (which was to become gradually more and more angular, more Germanic). Her eyes are gray/lavender/blue/green (is it that I don't remember? or is it that they also changed?). Quiet. The only woman who signed up for every mountain-climbing expedition. Had one scary mescaline trip a year before anyone else we knew. She didn't talk much about it. A photographer, a kid who wanted to be a photographer, taking pictures since she was fourteen. She always loved animals, and removed the stray caterpillars from the road.

(40)   Out of light-catching chemicals their images move. Hesitant and canny as winter fox they shatter the surface of their portraits, common as ripples they come toward us.

"Abby, my back is killing me. Fuck rehearsals anyway. Canya give me a backrub?" Peggy asks. Both of them lived in the low cinderblock new dorm which looked much like a World War I bunker. They were friends. Peggy had known some of Abby's relatives. They both took photographs.

It wasn't easy for Abby to make friends, because she talked so little (shy, they call it). It wasn't easy for Peggy to keep friends, because she could talk so much. They were naturals; they became friends. Dorms, the first or eighteenth time away from home, are desolate as solitary cells; it helps to move from room to room, to have friends with whom to break the rules.

Inez lived in a single in the old building and, as a senior and member of Student Court, had been assigned Abby's roommate, Delphine, as her counselee. She came down frequently, looking for Delphine, staying to listen to the Stones through Delphine's earphones. Peggy didn't like it one bit. And told Abby, "That Inez Riverfingers is a creep, I don't know why you sit still for her bullshit."

Abby was too polite to argue. Inez would come down looking for Delphine and sometimes stay overnight and Abby would always offer her bunk, roll out her sleeping bag and sleep on the floor. Inez was a big shot. Delphine and Inez had hitchhiked to New York and Washington—Delphine was a sexy juvenile delinquent, Inez a respectable child prodigy, together they were impressive women to be reckoned with. When they smoked dope together on campus they let Abby come along. Besides, Inez had very broad shoulders that Abby liked to watch, night after night, in assembly. *(41)*

One day in study hall Delphine told Abby that Inez was a queer—proof being that Inez had tried to sleep with her, Delphine. Abby had never known a queer before. Besides, there was something about Inez—her shoulders in assembly, among other things—that Abby liked to watch. All of which set Abby thinking. There were no real words yet to what she thought.

"Hey, Abby, what about that backrub?" Peggy asked again. Night study hall in the dorms. Abby was always on the honor roll, all her teachers liked her for being so quiet and prepared. A model student. She didn't have to stay in her room during study hall, but usually did. Peggy was sometimes on honor roll, when her teachers couldn't avoid putting her there, but none of them approved of her affectations or her sleeping around or that stuff about becoming an actress. Something about Peggy Warren offended their senses of propriety—even the youngest teachers were reluctant to give her A's when she deserved them. Delphine was never on honor roll.

"Okay, Peggy, lie down over there." It was study hall in the dorm and quiet.

"I'll take my blouse off. Take yours off and I'll give you a rubdown when you finish me."

"That'll be good." Abby sat on Peggy's ass to rub her back. Both of them had a sense that here they were, sixteen and seventeen, half-naked. Both of them had slept with men. Neither of them knew what to make of it. "This feel okay?"

"That feels fine, Abby." They rubbed each other's backs for a long time, first one, then the other. Sometimes their nipples touched each other's spines or shoulder blades (but they didn't know, they were afraid, they could neither shudder nor turn to each other with open palms). Then they were tired of rubbing. They lay on the single bed built into the dormitory wall, looking at the cinderblocks. Delphine had transformed the room as best she could with red lightbulbs, peacock feathers, posters of Black Panthers. Abby had put up her poster of horses.

They lay next to each other. Each wondered who was going to move first. Each knew it wouldn't be her. They were women, after all. Their thoughts were all unformed. They tried not to think at all about what was happening, to concentrate on breathing. No good—suddenly they were aware of the other's chest moving. They lay side by side, waiting, anxious.

A knock on the door. The dorm mother, naturally.

"What's going on here? This is a study hall. Why aren't you in your room, Peggy, and where's Delphine tonight?" The dorm mother was tired and a little angry.

They put on their blouses quickly. They knew she was as uptight about finding them there together as they were about being found. The dorm mother was only five years older than they were. Only Delphine had to be accounted for.

"She—I think she's with Inez, in the newspaper office. Natasha gave them permission," said Abby. (43)

"Natasha is *not* on duty in this dorm. I'm sick of her letting all you kids hide behind her." (Natasha was the young art teacher, Inez's first and only lasting mother surrogate, and the only person who had ever asked Inez about what it was in Inez that made her homosexual. Inez was shocked and frightened by her asking that, and then she came to have a crush on her, just like in all the books.) "Delphine gets away with murder on account of Natasha—talking to Inez, I bet!"

Door closes. Peggy and Abby never made love while they went to Highland. They didn't make love until the year that Abby and Inez were living together in Chicago—when Peggy was in the process of dropping out of the University of Colorado, a list of pricks as long as your arm stenciled between labia majora and labia minora.

Peggy and Abby, Abby and Peggy. Peggy *meant* to, even then. Peggy was very sure that she was a straight woman by that time, so a little bisexual experimentation, that would be all right, that wouldn't hurt her credentials. Peggy meant to, but we all know what a hard time women have making the first move.

Peggy had an idea about it though—it was a whole plan about how to escape what was happening to Peggy Warren and live a simpler life. Sometimes Abby, when she talked, would talk about how Abby was going to grow up and live in the mountains in Colorado, how she was going to build an octagonal cabin and live with her horses, how she always wanted to go to Colorado.

Conveniently, Peggy had some relatives in Boulder, who would help them find an apartment that very summer. Peggy and Abby would fly out to Boulder, and get an apartment, and there would just be the two of them, and no men who knew Peggy and wanted to lay her. It would just be Abby and Peggy then, and well, maybe something would happen.

"You know," Peggy told Inez, two, three years later in Chicago. "I had plans for Abby myself."

"No kidding."

"No kidding. Before you got into the picture I figured I'd sleep with Abby myself when we got to Colorado, and if it worked out okay, I wouldn't leave at all, I wouldn't bother to finish high school, or else I'd go out there."

"How come you never told us?"

"Aw, come on, Inez—all you and Abby ever did was make love. I have a lot of respect for young lovers myself. I figured you wouldn't want to know about it. Besides, remember? you didn't like me very well then."

"Yeah, I remember that. You're right. I wouldn't have wanted to know."

And that's all there was to high school. Come on now. That couldn't have been all there was to high school. Certainly there must have been classes. There must have been teachers. You must have studied something besides sexual fantasy and how to roll joints 101.   (45)

There were classes. Everyone knows what classes are. When your great aunt Violet asks you, "And what are you studying this year, dear?", you have to stand there and say, "Oh, the usual—Algebra, English, Frog Dissection, Gym," before she gives you the shiny new dollar bill she saves for budding scholars. I still cringe when people ask me what I got my degree in, I imagine myself tugging at a goatee and answering "Ah, hmph, actually, advanced animate orgasm and, uh, the biological ramifications of concrete poetry on the nervous systems of invertebrates, why do you ask?" At Highland Hills they occasionally had crazy Czechoslovakian refugees or beautiful people teaching economics and comparative religion. Even so, classes were still classes, and most of the time you could learn more getting stoned and staring at the ceiling.

We three—Inez, Peggy, Abby—were curious about knowledge. We had aspirations. In our own distinct adolescent ways we clawed at the sources available.

For Peggy it was the theater. Acting fascinated her. People talk a lot about actresses being actresses because they're always role-playing anyway, no way to get them to be real. But Peggy went into the theater because she wasn't good at acting at all. Every time she tried to play a role—running for Student Council, loyal girlfriend—it backfired. It was easier on stage, people can look at the part you're playing with the lines and action mapped out before them, and know you. People see immediately that all the characters on stage are interdependent and that someone else wrote the script. The players either do their job or they don't; beyond that, there's no way to fault them. So Peggy studied theater and was in every play they did at Highland.

Abby was more practical. She was best at geometry, she began to draw the plans for her cabin, and the men teachers would help her figure it out. She was better still at hiking. All the other girls in the rec room would watch her lace her big hiking boots and go off, day after day, to bring back dozens of rocks in her pockets. Sometimes she went to the Friday night dances held in the dining room; Peggy and Delphine (her roommate) always went, but more often she stayed in her room and read.

She didn't like to call attention to herself, beyond lacing up her hiking boots in the rec room. Besides, the problem of whether or not the boys liked her (and whether or not she liked them) was embarrassing in front of Peggy and Delphine, because every junior prick in school wanted to lay *them*.

Of course, there was music. Hard Rock with the Guru Beat. The Beatles came out with "Revolver," the Stones did "Between the Buttons" in time for Christmas shoppers, Jefferson Airplane cut "Surrealistic Pillow," the Doors made "The Doors" and Inez lost her virginity while hearing Buffalo Springfield for the first time. Sometimes we listened to Judy Collins or Joan Baez, but we felt a little silly doing it. Women folksingers are okay for mood music, but they ain't the real thing, the boys said. The boys knew. After all, they invented rock music, invented all the 'babby ooo wa i gotta gotta gotta have it whadya say sleep with me tonight my ooo wa diddle dee dum back street baaaaaby.' *(47)*

There were the teachers themselves. A lot of young adults and middle-aged adults and old adults wanting to instruct us. We treated them with the fear that had been bred in us, which they mistook for respect. Some were anxious to be our friends, which meant they wanted to have influence. So we went to them when someone had run away from school or was overdosing on speed or smoking dope too openly on campus, and they would help us. In the spirit of molding youth. They also helped girls get their first abortions and birth control pills, when girls had courage enough to ask them.

Some teachers found themselves being confidants without really meaning to be, or at least, without knowing what they were getting into. Natasha Riverfingers was one of those. Her husband, Rananum, enjoyed influence and attention; girls fought over a ride downhill on the English teacher's Harley. But Natasha was just trying to do what she was paid for, and wasn't clear on exactly what that was. She was about twenty-four and a painter, very tall, thin, and beautiful. She found Inez interesting, and when Abby came, she liked Abby, though she never had good feelings toward Peggy and Delphine. Inez talked about free will and art and being an artist and destiny with Natasha. Inez sought Natasha out and said, "Nobody understands me, all I want is a horse and a zither and a cabin in the woods." Natasha would indulge her for a while, then say, "Cut it out, Inez, we all know you wouldn't know how to get on a horse if you ever saw one."

Inez wanted to grow up to be an intellectual. She read a lot of heavy books that men had written which her teachers were delighted to give her. Going to classes was not her style exactly, but she did spend night after night researching Keynes' economic systems and Pound's poetic theory, so her teachers let her do whatever she wanted. What she wanted was power. She had a sense that it wasn't going to be easy for her, a fat crazy queer, if she didn't learn a little self-protection.

There's a glitter in how things run: she wanted to know the tricks, the ropes, the ins and outs, the way to influence, the art of manipulation—as much as she could, being female. Her teachers were delighted to have such a perceptive student.

In the meantime, Peggy also was learning about manipulation. Peggy sat on Student Council. To Peggy, there was something attractive about being public. And she, too, understood the need to protect yourself if you're gonna be a loose woman.

Inez and Peggy each saw that the other was getting an education in influence, and although each of them wanted to learn how to get what she wanted, neither of them wanted to be manipulated herself. They were very wary of the people who were good at the same things they were.

Abby, on the other hand, voted for Inez and she voted for Peggy, because she knew who they were. She walked in the woods with her camera. I try to picture you, to see you walking, Abby, clearing the pine boughs in front of you, turning to see your tracks in the Berkshire snow. When did you learn to use your eyes like that?

There with her camera, silent in the woods, the beauty of things naked as breath pressed against her shutter. And then back to the dark room to find a precise way to reveal her vision. Abby didn't like to talk much, she didn't know what to say, but she wanted to be heard, she wanted other people to see what she saw. Possibly the only person who understood was Natasha. Abby didn't show her pictures much, but she would sometimes walk the two miles to Natasha and Rananum's house to show them what she had done in the darkroom and Natasha always gave her and Delphine lunch (even though Delphine only came along for the chance to smoke a joint on the walk).

Inez didn't catch Abby's developing vision. Inez was full of herself. It was about time for full women in the world, and Inez was working on it, political things, ways of influence, writing. She didn't have much time yet for real trees or real leaves or rocks or anyone else's sense of vision. She knew that Abby was a good photographer, she'd seen the pictures on Abby's desk, but it was a point of information.

When she was doing the yearbook, at the end of the year, she needed a photographer, remembered about Abby's pictures, and used Abby. They went around together, taking pictures to fill the blank spaces in Inez's layout, and Inez began to grasp the mechanics of basic photography. It was only a long time later, pointing her finger and seeing Abby's picture or trying to figure out just what it was Abby was aiming at, that she realized how Abby had slowly given her a real sense of real leaves and real trees and real nature, had opened up vision—but that's ahead of what we learned in high school.

(50)

We smoked a lot of marijuana and found out everything we could about sex and fucking and the free love through our fantasies and fumbling with each other. We wondered if anyone would ever come who would love us. We tried to figure out Existentialism and wondered if our bodies could really be as ugly as we thought they were. That's all there was to high school.

Meanwhile, the powers that be have not been sleeping. There are agents. There are undercover policemen. There is a committee. And they have been watching. They follow up on these things. It's one matter, after all, for kids to be kids, even girls, these days, if they come from broken families, and it's quite another to engage in antipaternal writing and smuggling in hashish from Tangiers without the right connections.

The committee is not at all sure that they like Inez Riverfingers. They are getting together a preliminary report.

A man comes to Natasha Riverfingers' door, in early 1971. He says he's a reporter for the local underground paper. She has no reason not to believe him. She invites him in for coffee. Inez has had some stories printed lately, he wants to talk to her about Inez. She says she doesn't have much time, but he can stay a little while, as long as the children are napping. She is not sure how helpful she can be.

"But you've read what Inez has written, haven't you? I mean, you've known her for—six years, is it?"

"Yes, six years I think."

"So you've been able to watch her writing develop?"

"Well, I'm not a writer. I still think her sense of dialogue is a little—shallow, I guess, but I wouldn't really want to—make a judgment about it."

"Well, let me ask you this, then, Mrs. Riverfingers. We hear she's writing a book—she calls it a—pornographic novel. Have you read it?"

"No, I haven't. I expect to when Inny comes East again."

"You still keep in touch?"

(51)

"Oh, of course. She comes here about once a year, sometimes twice, to visit and play with the children. She's their godmother, you know."

"That must be very nice for you."

"Well, I like it. We haven't always made life easy for each other, but I feel very close to her. We have pretty open wavelengths. You know, it isn't very easy for me to talk to you. What is it you want to know anyway?"

"Oh, I'm just writing an article on the new women writers—you know, a lot more women are getting published and read, and I'm just doing some background research on them."

"I see."

"Are you active in the women's movement, Mrs. Riverfingers?"

"No. I'm not very interested in politics. I leave that pretty much up to my husband. I know that's anachronistic, but I enjoy being a little different from my friends."

"Uh huh. Now, I understand, from my sources, that Inez is writing about some kind of smuggling operation in Tangiers. Do you know if that's first hand information, I mean, is that the kind of thing she's been involved in in the past?"

"No idea. It's an interesting thought, though. It would be a little surprising, I think. Inny? Well, maybe—can't tell what kind of people she's been hanging around with lately. I would think she wouldn't do that kind of stuff seriously, but you never know."

"I'm curious, Mrs. Riverfingers—"

"You can call me Natasha."

"Okay. Natasha. I was curious about the kind of relationship you have with Inez, if that's not too personal to ask about?"

"I really don't like talking about my life very much."

"Well, I'll try to practice a little discretion . . . Do you know that Inez is a homosexual?"

"Who doesn't? Inny has a real talent for confession."

"Hmm. Well, have you found that her—problem —has affected your relationship?"

"I don't see it as a problem. I thought she might grow out of it, but it's very stylish now, you know."

"I thought you said you weren't involved in the women's movement?"

"I'm not. But that doesn't stop me from thinking. Inny and I have talked about it, but she's been getting more defensive lately."

"Defensive how?" (53)

"Well, we're just going in very different directions right now. That's all."

"You mean, her being involved in the gay subculture and you having a family?"

"I guess you could put it like that."

"Have you found, I guess this is what I was asking before, that her—I guess we don't call it deviation any more?"

"No."

"Well, that she's cast you in the role of a mother figure, or else has some kind of—physical attraction towards you?"

"I think that's a little personal."

"Well, Mrs. Riverfingers—uh, Natasha, let me

ask this: Have you ever had any homosexual—relationships?"

"No. That's a little personal too."

"It's interesting that you should think so. Seems like everyone's really eager to talk about their sexuality these days. Well, why do you think someone like Inez is interested in maintaining a friendship with someone like yourself, considering, as you yourself said, that your lives are going in such different directions?"

"We've been friends a long time. We always have a lot to talk about with each other. It's quiet here, for her, she can read, she can play with the children. She's always liked children. There aren't a whole lot of people that I enjoy talking with—I think Inez knows that, and appreciates what I give her."

"And what's that?"

"What I've just said. Listen, I think that's about all I can tell you, and I have a lot of people coming over for dinner, so I think I'd like to end now, if that's all right with you."

"Let me see—oh yes, I just wanted to check out one more thing. In this—uh, novel she's writing, Inez says that she had a relatively long relationship with a girl that she met at boarding school, a girl you knew too. I just wanted to know if the relationship lasted as long as she said it did, to know how reliable her other facts are—homosexual relationships are notoriously very brief. It's rare that we hear of one lasting six months, let alone three years, especially among such young girls."

"Did she say it lasted three years?"

"Yes."

"Well, actually, maybe it was two and a half. Are you done now?"

"Yes, I think I've asked all the questions I can think of—that you'd answer, anyway. Thank you very much, Mrs. Riverfingers."

°

Oh, Natasha, didn't you ever think that it was a little suspicious for an underground newspaper to send out a man to write about women?

As I did my star paintings and wrote:

>and her flesh crawled
>with stars;
>her armpits
>bred stars;
>her name was written
>in stars;
>we have spoken of stars;
>should we not
>reach for her?

I thought: they will accuse me of sexism again, for using a woman—the "universal she"—as a symbol, unnameable and detached. Women suffer from this continually in the hands of art, this mythness which denies the oneness of each of them, and makes them separate, jealous and remote. (59)

But I also am a woman. I know that there is a mucous to each of us, childhood scabs, wrinkles in the flesh—and more than that, a singular blossom and singular decay and life that has something to do with ironing boards and afterbirth, shopping carts and potting soil (all the trivials, that make up everybody's day). The unnameable persists, nonetheless.

It persists in men, who have managed to make much more comfortable pedestal myths for themselves—teacher and saviour and god myths.

Now it's my turn. I want to get my women, I mean not the actual living breathing people who work hard and sweat, but the dream of my women,

the world where all women are strong and beautiful, even me—I want to get my women to be
bullfighters, as well as those slivers that men trace
between the silver and the gold. I want my women
to be Amazons and perfect truck drivers, weight
lifters and cross-country runners.

I made it a woman I reach for in the stars because
it *is* a woman. As I come to grips with that there are
less generalizations, and the sprouting of specific
arms starts (their freckles, the vaccination marks,
my cheekbones cool against them). There remains a
richness yet in the myth which cannot be denied
without diminishing the quality of our fucking-
belching utilitarian lives. The vision of who we are
and who we can be, a race of intact human beings
unafraid to give to each other, one to one, in
specific ways, and more than one to one, in groups,
in the new ways we are learning. To give, each
time, the vision of each woman.

(60)

And this woman is of course myself—and this
hand is my own and these stars are ink from the
bottles by my bed, and the sheets are covered with
ink tonight and Hubert Humphrey was on the radio
just now, talking about the Russians.

These are the titles of the large star paintings that
I made when I was alone and waiting:

"Their hands passed: pyramids of the sky"

"Taurus—the Woman in the Ring"

"How many shooting stars?"

"She makes a picture of the big dipper from
memory"

"Now I am going to sleep"

"Is it morning yet?"

Leave us some nitty gritty, for god's sake. They made love, didn't they? What's it like for two women to make love?

Pretty much as you would expect.

○

This is an excerpt from the official recruitment pamphlet, *Meet Today's WAC Officer*:

You're naturally curious about a WAC officer's life—and if you're like most women, one of your first questions is "What will I be wearing?"

[USARCAI-D   15 March 1974   *(61)*

Miss Elana Nachman
200 Main Street
Northampton, Massachusetts 01060

Dear Miss Nachman:

Reference is made to your letter of February 15, 1974 requesting permission to use a paragraph from a WAC recruiting brochure in your novel. Your request was directed to the legal advisor for this Command, who determined that you may use the material in question.

Your interest in the United States Army is appreciated.

       Sincerely,

       PETER N. LEONE, II
       Lieutenant Colonel, GS
       Chief, Advertising Distribution Division]

Time and Peggy shuttle in and out continually. Peggy is by far the most interesting of us. With Bruce (who looks not unlike Charlie Manson, albeit handsomer, in the photograph I have of him, which is sitting on top of an old Carnation ice-cream container and resting against the yellow windowshade in the kitchen) who pimped for her in Paris. Who died of an o.d. beside her in Tangier (which set off the incredible hashish smuggle). With our own orgies in my grandmother's living room, under the portrait of my great-grandfather (may he have gotten a little excitement in those hydabed gymnastics), our long talks in gay bars.

Peggy, Peggy I have been hard at work on my pornographic novel for three days now when the hell are you going to get here? Do you think I can actually do justice to your life and everyone else's lust with just the handful of experience I have outside my two year monogamy with Abby?

Why is no one ever around when I need them?

°

Pretty much as you would expect. The first love between women. Inez and Abby.

Inez had begun to be aware of Abby on the periphery of everything she was doing. Inez was trying to get out the school yearbook with another student. They needed more pictures for it. All the boys who took photographs were generally incompetent, besides being impossible to work with. Inez remembered that Delphine's roommate took good pictures. Peggy Warren took pictures too, she remembered, but Peggy Warren wouldn't want to work with her, so she asked this quiet girl who seemed like she wouldn't give Inez a hard time, who seemed like she could take direction: Abby.

Abby said fine. Inez arranged to get Abby out of most of her classes for a week (Inez had just then reached the peak of getting what she wanted by manipulation).

It is really a very simple story, our courtship. Chimpanzees circling on their haunches, sniffing each other's asses. Does the spider love its mate, with its sticky web and dangling fate?

Innocent movie of Greek restaurant eating contests and barefoot races in the middle of the city, first love, true love, is it love? how will we decode what we are saying to each other?

Shall our hair blow in the lilac wind crossing a meadow, too shy (too scared shitless) to take each other's hand? The chimps get a little closer with their noses.

Here's the first postcard Inez wrote Abby from Baltimore (Inez's home town) over Easter vacation:

(63)

> I ask only
> that Oblivion, a bride heavy with censure,
> should grant me this:
> to be an epicure in my small delights,
> a dilettante in how I choose
> my mistresses.

But Abby thought it was a sign of sure rejection, that she was not the mistress Inez would choose. There is this continual problem, that we are all speaking our separate language without interpreters, especially in these delicate matters.

Then there was a scene in Natasha's house, in the woods, where we went together one night, to cook dinner for Rananum while Natasha was out of town. It was an honor, back in those days, to be able to cook dinner for your English teacher.

But we were too flustered to do it. We kept bumping into each other when we turned around in the small kitchen, and giggling. Finally Rananum cooked his own hamburger and left us there, while he went to a rehearsal at the school theater.

Now we are alone here. We search around the house for some grass, but all we can find are seeds, because Rananum and Natasha have their stash well hidden. They couldn't afford any more rumors about what went on in their house than there were already. We crushed the seeds and smoked them anyway.

Abby put Bob Dylan on; words larded with sexual innuendo filled the narrow gap of our silence. Abby said later she was trying to tell me something. I was sitting on the arm of the chair she was sitting in. Four times I moved my hand to just above her head, as if (as if!) to touch her hair. I couldn't. I wasn't hearing the message she was sending clearly, but then again, something in me heard. I wanted then to know if Abby "knew"—if someone had told her that she was hanging out with a dangerous person. That would indicate, at least, that she might be interested. This is how I tried to find out:

"Hey, Abby—do you know who Alice B. Toklas was?"

"Nope."

"Well, uh—did Delphine ever tell you about the time me and her went to Washington, what happened?"

"Not much."

"Oh."

Rananum came back and drove us to the dorms.

There follows a sequence where Inez and Abby run away for a day. Hands in pockets, they are whistling stoned down the dirt road to an abandoned summer camp: there is no one in the world but us now.

"Look," Abby said, on the porch of the old bunk that had no windows, and huge gaps in its side. "There's a river in the sky." A river in the sky. Just for us dear little Riverfinger children. We buzz around all day in each other's strawberry field vision.

"Abby, if we stay here, we'll have to build a fire. And maybe—Rananum told me this story, that when he was on a mountain climbing trip and there was snow and they had not brought warm enough things with them, they survived by—sleeping together—for, you know, body heat. So what d'you think—you think we should go back?" Another coded proposition.

"I don't know if we should stay or not," said Abby.

"Well, you decide. You're oldest." Abby laughed at that and started gathering fire wood. The sun was going down. We had a cup of yogurt and a ten cent package of doughnuts, for dinner. And still I couldn't tell if she was saying what I wanted her to say. Did building a fire mean: Yes, we will stay, I want you, or: Yes, we'll stay, it's an adventure, but I don't want to hear any more of this body-heat crap?

It is colder than I could have imagined. Abby, Abby? Hold me. Warm me. I have wanted this for so long. I am not sure I want this at all. I don't know what I'm doing here. I keep talking. Tear the

(65)

words out of my mouth like hooks that have lodged in a fish gill.

Years pass. My feet turn blue in the May chill. It is Gemini. Exhausted I lay my head in Abby's lap and have the dream of the gold earrings.

"Are you awake already? Can't your sleep?" Abby wonders what all this wondering is. This nervousness. Wants what Inez does, waits for Inez to do it first, just as ready to say, no, it isn't anything, it wasn't anything. She was so close to this girl they said wanted to sleep with other women. She had already slept with men, that had been all right, but nothing special. The female closeness was different. She began to think what it might be like, wanting to sleep with other women. She had this friend she liked to be with, whom she knew wanted to sleep with women. Abby had muscles but she had been brought up a woman like the rest of us, to be solicitous of her friends. Here was a friend who wanted something. Abby was not afraid to ask herself if she could give it, if she could also want it. To ask yourself is not the same as answering out loud. She had been secretly looking at the pictures of women in magazines, to see if she liked women's bodies, if they excited or pleased her. That was a way, she thought, to find out, because men always looked at women's bodies in magazines and they must see something pleasing. So she began to look, wondering if she was pleased. When she watched Inez from the back in assembly she didn't wonder, she knew. To know inside yourself at seventeen is not the same as saying it out loud. The closeness she had with her friend was important to her, it would endanger that closeness to say either *no* or *yes*. Inez had her head on Abby's lap. That pleased Abby, and was a comfort in the deserted summer camp in the woods. Knowing that Inez was only interested in women was also a comfort. Delphine and Peggy were Abby's friends, but they did the honky tonk with boys, and it was doubtful that either of them would end up with their heads in her lap, that they would bring their restlessnesses to be nourished by Abby. With Inez there was a new kind of certainty. Both of them were totally present, both wanted to have this adventure in the cold May night. Abby hadn't had that feeling since she was a child. Friends together, totally absorbed in play, openly liking how close they were. She wished Inez had kept her head down long enough for her to begin to touch it.

"But I was asleep. I just had this—wow—I just had this amazing dream that you gave me a pair of gold earrings that cost eighty-seven dollars and you made them yourself and they were more beautiful than anything else ever made in the world."

"But your eyes were only closed for a few seconds, Inez,"

Another miracle dream. A sign.

It's just as well. Now she is sure I'm awake and I'm sure it is not merely her kindness. Our hands reached and met in the fire-smoke. Where did you learn this? Where did you learn to do this dance with your fingers? (When did you come to want me?) Is this what sex is? this nod and play and rub of pinky to thumb and index to ring finger, this dance in the cold, by the fire, making shadows of animals in the darkness? This gentle friction that is more sexual than anything I have ever known? Where in god's name did you learn this?

○

"You're not going to tell me that you didn't make love, even then?"

"I am going to tell you just that. I've been trying to explain how inhibiting it's been to be a homosexual in America."

○

Between fear and not enough fire there was no room for sleep. When the dawn came we tried to put out the fire—no good. So we left it burning slowly, trembling before a frowning, growling Smokey the Bear of Conscience.

Walked jumping up and down in the cold bright green pastures by streams where fish grew silverfat after the winter meltings, back to school.

(68)   Harold (the headmaster, Theodora's loyal son) had found out they were missing, and had called Natasha, thinking they might have gone there. Natasha, who was not used to being uninformed when Inez was going to need her to cover for her, began to worry. She went to campus and found Delphine. Delphine told Natasha that we couldn't have gone very far, because she, Delphine, was at that moment somehow in possession of both our money *and* our dope—so—maybe—and then Delphine looked at Natasha, and Natasha thought, well, maybe they are out falling in love with each other somewhere. It surprised her that both she, Natasha, and Delphine (whom she couldn't stand) should have the same insight. So she went to Harold and persuaded him that he shouldn't call

their parents or the police until the morning. He had been living in a boarding school since he was a little boy and now he was a middle-aged man. He waited.

When they came into his office he called them in separately, in order to scare them better, and also to see if an act of—coercion (or something. He had no idea what a lesbian was, but he knew that they said Inez was one, he had *seen* enough to know that she was, but he didn't believe it of Abby, and he was just checking) hadn't taken place. Finally he shrugged them off with a sigh, it being only three weeks until graduation, saying:

"If only you could have called!" No phone, Harold.

Abby slept. I went to a party at Natasha's and Natasha not only did not try to convince me that I was once again on the brink of ruining my life because my crotch went thump thump when I (69) watched her leaning out the window or lacing up her boots (which it did, thump) but was even pleased enough to see me that she forgave us for keeping them up all night with worry. It was very reassuring to me then, to have this grown woman not insist (although she secretly believed it) that I'd grow out of it.

Jesus, Inez, a voice in my head said before I fell asleep in Natasha's bedroom, maybe you are doing the right thing. Those nights with your arms curved around your own thickness saying to yourself, "I will be enough for myself—I will never need anyone. Never. I will be for myself, warm and all"—are those times gone?

Those times are now, dammit.

How will I say what happened then? It is four a.m. Peggy is lost or busted somewhere in the midwest. Abby is in Israel.

Will Peggy make the deal? Will Abby come back? Will the hash arrive without hitch? Will sex role stereotyping die a natural death? What did Holly do with the four hundred dollars? Is the committee closing in? Will we impeach Nixon? Are adolescents still going through these things? I have no answers to the questions you think I have answers for. I have been a secretary, folded lingerie in department stores, been a short order cook, dope peddler and thief, but I have never written a novel before: start where the tap is running and proceed.

Invent, imagine, saw apart the lady in the big pine box! You have the power, yours the keys, do away with dead wood, bring back your dreams, come on kid, we know you can. Endings, middles, finish lines, pass go, shuffle on along to Buffalo.

Ten days before graduation in 1967 I wrote Abby a note: I have one paper left to write, come tomorrow night if you want to sleep with me. If you want, I wrote, we can keep on our clothes.

Abby came that afternoon. She sat close to me on my bed, and instead of touching her we talked about Asoka, king of India in 273 B.C.

I never wrote the last paper. We went back to my room after dinner. I remember thinking: but the note said *tomorrow* night. I wanted to wash my hair first, to shave my legs, to smell right.

Does it begin here? When somehow whatever was between us—book or paper, fear, ideas—is suddenly gone and our hands move over each other's shirts and our hands begin that amazing dance they started in the woods and our mouths search for their sister along the pathways of the neck, the cheek, the ticklish earlobes, the forehead, the nose, infinite search for the mouth of its lover, tastebuds playing in a field of eyebrow, tip out now for the mouth of its sister, of its mother, of its child, of its father (we have always known that the woman is supposed to let the man's tongue run and rub in the dark between her rows of teeth, her tongue beneath his) but we are equals here, now both of us have to learn how to give—whose tongue goes where? Great joyful awkwardness, a slow disturbance of the wound. Abby! Is it the law of averages, that out of a thousand fantasies one should come true? Are you happy? Yes, yes, I have never been so happy, I have never been.   (71)

Heavy hairy legs why haven't I tamed you for the pleasure of my lover? Could I have thought she'd never come? Easily.

Dorm mothers agree to let Abby stay with Inez (innocent desire of young girls to giggle up together telling stories all night in separate corners).

"We won't say that we love each other, it's too corny. Okay? There are only ten days left. We will only say what it is. We are enjoying each other, that's all, right?"

"Right," Abby said. There was at first not much talking.

We undressed, we took our fingers out of dancing school and started them in on finger-painting lessons of the skin. That first night rolling with each other, kissing, small-paw first expeditions to the breast (the breast!) finally to touch them after years of wanting, to woo them with fur and jewels, soft lips, warm tongue; to take her nipples in the sundance month of my new mouth, as her hand stroked my hair and moved down my shoulders, poking in my sides, every inch of me shuddered, confounded and pleased by her responsiveness, her own desire. I followed with fingers like young white colts, tracing the globe of ass, mimicking it with sphere of palm, keeping the record player on, keeping time with the music (pack up, that time is gone) singing to each other in shy dandelion voices, reaching orgasm after orgasm by the mere shock of it to each of us, our bodies on top of each other, too uncertain even then about how to send our fingers to graduate school—the warm halls of vagina, mysterious and still frightening then. The sun comes up and miracle—she is here still, not vanished or turned to heap of wheat in the dawn.

(72)

That, anyway, is how Inez would describe it. Abby, did you feel the same?

"I felt the same, but I wouldn't have described it. You know, when you first sucked my breasts, that surprised me—it turned me off a little, because I didn't expect it. But then I liked it. I liked it a lot."

No one seemed to bother us. It was only ten nights. Natasha may have covered for us ("Natasha, I have something to tell you. You know that night me and Abby were in the woods, and how she is sleeping in my room now, I—" "It's all right, Inez," Natasha said. "I know, and I think it's nice."). Maybe the authorities just didn't care.

During that time we left young nuzzledom only twice voluntarily. Natasha took me to Boston, where I could only stumble, dazed, buying presents: a knife with a fine-grain wood handle, a Japanese dragon kite to hang across the room. This is for you. Everything is for you, Abby. Years of single beds, nights of fists clenched against the moon—for you. Birds that cannot contain their joy that the world has turned successfully again—for you. All motion, all madness, all glee, all regret—I have no claims on the world, it is yours, I am yours, a bundle of nerves and muscle, the Loch Ness monster whinnying at the pleasure wave, a fan of emerald feathers the Emperor of China gave for the deepest dew-crazed sigh, I am not going anywhere, I wanted to wander, hunkering after love, but it is here, are you going to Colorado, Abby, can I come?

And once, because she was a little more calm than I, or because it was all new in her, something (73) she had not been quite ready for from her silence and the watching and wanting she had before it really happened, Abby took her walking stick to prod the mud holes of that late mountain spring, while Inez sat on the fire escape, writing poems (when you are the mountains and come to me . . .). Abby returned clear-eyed and humming; she had seen the tadpoles, and had decided it was fine to be caught up in the middle of this sexual energy, being how it was 1967 and come on baby.

All things of the earth that run and jump, that skip and hop, that glide, slide, run, ride walk crawl roll or swim, that creep soar, climb or leap into the sun are friends of our slow, dazed journey, our week-long Spanish conquistador expedition with banners and jade bridles, tambourines and drums, our treasure hunt toward each other's cunts. (Cunts! What harsh words this language has for the most delicate parts of its own flesh. Who gave us these words, anyway? But those are the words we use these days; either reclaim them or let the men keep them. Okay. I announce the beauty of our cunts, the gleaming brown of them, their full rights and privileges as citizens of our bodies.)

It took our hands awhile to get that far, to find that art, but we drew closer and closer, and each new closeness, each new chance, made us happier than we had ever imagined from all the books and classes we had studied (as if there were a conspiracy to keep knowledge of pleasure from us). We spent four hours just in the bath one afternoon, kneading each other's stomachs with our feet, outlining the jaw with big toe, gently now, go easy, moving the soap up and down—ribs and shoulders and pelvic region, necks and knuckles and the small ridge under the breast, hers small, mine big.

(74)

°

In high school it was not very fashionable to acknowledge that you had parents. Better to be an orphan, formed from the dust of the nuclear age, than to suffer the shame of normal origin. Even Inez Riverfingers had parents, though she had left them at fourteen. She made it explicit how dangerous it was, them living in one house; she tried repeatedly and seriously to kill herself. The doctors said it was an adolescent adjustment reaction (lot of girls have these problems when it's time for them to stop being one of the gang and start dating; they usually get over it and get into stockings easier than Inez, though, the doctors said). Inez's parents were well-educated second and third generation Americans just a little left of liberal, and they wanted to do right by their kids. They were cowed by their daughter's actions and her psychiatrists' explanations, and they were ready to follow instructions. Inez had risked her life to get away from them, she was tough, and the doctors said the toughness would get her by, for all her sensitivity. Better to let her live on her own, in halfway houses and boarding schools. Reluctantly they let her go.

Mr. and Mrs. Bramanoi came to the graduation of their daughter, Inez. Mr. Bramanoi's sister, Aunty Tilly, came, and his second cousin Ruth (fifteen) who was close to them. Mrs. Bramanoi's mother came, Rose (in whose New York apartment a great deal of dope had been smoked). Inez was Rose's favorite grandchild. They came for the graduation. It was the least they could do. *(75)*

Inez's mother came to her room, while Inez was packing her things, to give her a string of pearls for graduation. "They look very nice on you dear," her mother said. Inez looked at her mother then, a tall sophisticated woman who went to the beauty parlor every week. "Thanks, Mom," she said, and let her mother clasp the pearls around her neck, and wore a white dress to her graduation.

"Can my friend Abby come with us, out to dinner?" Inez asked then.

"Of course. It's your graduation, dear." The great graduation of Inez Riverfingers. Her parents were waiting, her parents hoped she would get an award—for the newspaper or the yearbook or being third in her class. But old Theodora had found Inez out: smoking dope in her room, with sophomores, no less. She said, "You must hate us very much now to do such a thing." Inez was sorry then, because she liked the old lady, so she pleaded confusion. "Theodora, I am having trouble with my sexual identity." Theodora had once met Freud, back in Vienna. She didn't kick Inez out of school but—no awards.

Mr. Bramanoi told stories of his own first days going to college, how *he* had needed scholarships and a job in a night kitchen, to get through school, being the son of an immigrant merchant. How his good wife had put him through law school, and then gave up a profession in journalism herself, to have children and look after him in his new career. He hoped much happiness for Inez, he did wish she had chosen a college closer to home—Oregon is a long way, he said. He said, Well, that's all right now, eat up.

Abby listened to Inez's parents very politely. They remarked on what a nice friend Inez had, how pleasant it would be for them to spend some time together in Colorado, how good to be close to nature, and go hiking in the mountains. Abby was very well-mannered and shy in front of them. A good trait in a woman, Mr. Bramanoi remarked to Inez afterward.

Inez had kicked her black heels off under the table, and was rubbing her foot up and down Abby's leg, between the varicose veins of her grandmother and Aunt Tilly. They were amusing each other very much, under the lace. They were careful to look the other way, so that no light might go forth and startle the young cousin or the waiter with the cheese pie.

Abby also had parents. They were good German Jewish people who lived on Long Island. Her father was president of a firm that was making a lot of money in New York City. Like many of his generation, he prided himself on being an honest, hard-working man. Her mother was working also; not because she needed to (she was quick to point out) but to be doing something good for people as a social worker. Abby was their youngest daughter, and Abby was already almost grown. Abby's father and mother went on with their lives and their work, all of which they regarded as part of the natural cycle that gave life meaning. Their oldest daughter had given them their first grandchild that year, and they were satisfied that their family life was secure.

Abby's parents also liked Inez, because she was another good Jewish girl, going on to college and well-mannered at the table. Abby's mother said to Abby, "You know, Inez would be a very beautiful girl if she would just lose weight—maybe you can help her a little, when you spend the summer in Colorado." Abby promised her mother to take good care of Inez.

They would begin to play as soon as Abby's parents left the house, every morning of the three

(77)

days they stayed there together. A kidhoodship of
sexual insanity starting at eight a.m. and lasting
until they were sure they'd get caught if they didn't
get dressed right then.

Peggy Warren—remember Peggy Warren?—
called to find out the final plans for going to
Colorado. It wasn't until then that Abby told her
Inez was coming too. Peggy had figured as much,
and said, Well, if she can stand me, I can stand her.
Then hung up. We ran the telephone receiver up
each other's thighs and into our crotches—just for a
few cool plastic minutes. We were careful to wipe it
off, so the smell wouldn't bother Abby's mom.

We fed each other marijuana brownies. We had
started in on the warehouse of taste, apple and
chocolate clinging to the creased lip skin and
flicked off with the tongue again, ending in long
kisses. Spelunking in the limestone cavern of the
mouth. Inez made up a song which she called "In
Praise of Oral Fixations, Among Other Things" and
it went like this:

(78)

> My fingers are dunked in whiskey and honey—
> they drum on your cunt,
> they cuddle your tummy.
> My mouth is a jug of mellow brandy—
> your mouth in mine
> is better than candy.
> My nipples are cider that never sours—
> both of us suck
> and forget the hours.
> Hungry women sing this song—
> Hungry women aren't hungry long.
> Strong women with appetites
> use their teeth but never bite,
> and kiss goodnight.

"Inez?" Ah, Abby, your eyelids, your hairline, the bone-fuzz of your cheek. *When* will you break our pact and say you love me?

"Uh-huh?" Lick. Maul. Mold. Rubadubdub two kids in a tub. Etc.

"Inez, I love you. I'm sorry, but I had to say it." Pshew. Old big swing bandmen sway your batons! Every angel in heaven and hell sends us a sideways wink.

"Oh, Abby, I thought you'd never say it. Should I start in now about the stars and the sun and the moon, the moon, the moon now? I love you too, I love you so much—"

"Hey, hey—take it easy, bum. Don't get all mushy on me. Oh, I don't care. I love you." Higgledy piggledy my true love set across the world in a foxskin glove. Here's where sapphire houses a rainbow of nonsense doves. Higgledy, piggledy, my true love. (79)

This is for you. Shhh. Suck hard. Touch here. Be slow. We have reached each other's ease. We are each other's children now, we will bring each other out of the uterus fresh, with only an infinite tenderness, a great chin-grin on the jaw of the speckled red doe who watches us from behind her curtain of leaves. Clear water, clear eyes, clean hands, pure crystal warm wet crotch—watch this— how many fingers do you think'll fit?

In my true love I could fit a fist.

Abby began to talk, began to tell all the names she had for herself, began to make up stories in bed, began to risk saying out loud what her memories were, what her life was inside, what her dreams had been. Called herself: Ali Bum Bar of the Orygun

Mists, Miss Quivnoss Something and Squid, Fearless Fosdick, Leche Fresca, Lucy Bear, Nikkos—the first secret name she named herself in childhood, Nikkos of the long fingers, perched in a tree branch for whole days, making up the guided tour speech of the ants: "And here we have our friendly child giant, Nikkos of the golden eyelash! Ho! Watch out! Don't get too close!"—and off the ant tour goes, in search of a vegetable garden.

Nikkos the good had a small hairline up her belly from mound to button, with a few extra-long hairs Inez tried to pull, obnoxious as any late adolescent.

"Listen, Inez, my belly button has just been declared a de-militarized zone. Make love, not war."

Once Inez managed to pull one out anyway ("ow, goddammit") and kept it encased in scotch tape for months before she lost it.

It is hard to believe that Inez Riverfingers, worried driver of a '61 International panel truck, ever knew these things. Just a few days ago Charles Bukowski (the pig poet) gave her a quick once over and said:

"And you! Writing a pornographic novel! Why I bet you haven't balled more than three times in six months, I bet you don't have anything to write about! Why don't you reduce and get some experience so you can write something you know about first hand! Look at the way she's staring at me! I bet you'd like to fuck me right now!"

Okay, Chuck, you still wanna bet?

Let us return to Peggy Warren, who was having a hard time, in the beginning of the last chapter, dealing with this interloper, this intruder, Inez Riverfingers. Finally she decided to go with Abby anyway, as they had planned; certainly Colorado would be cooler than New York City in the summertime. Maybe she would meet a rich cowboy and get married and settle down with a home on the range.

"Boy, did I hate you then!" Peggy said in a small bar on the East Side about two years ago. "All summer long, what did I have to listen to, day and night? Your fucking screams of orgasm."

"Now, come on, Peggy," Inez said. "It didn't take you more than ten days to start sleeping with the landlord's buddy, just back from exploring the Arctic. Besides, you could have joined us, if you'd really wanted to."

(81)

"Wait a second there. I tried. I would sit on your bed rapping for hours while you made out. I nearly drooled all over you. You just didn't want company."

We have been having this conversation for years. Meanwhile, there was Peggy, sitting on the edge of our bed in Colorado, rapping and rapping.

Peggy Warren sits on the edge of our bed
and tells her story:
or
What Peggy did before she came to Highland Hills

His name was Ross. He came from the same suburb that Peggy and Abby's relatives came from. Peggy passed up a chance of going to Scotland on scholarship to live with him for a year, even though he slammed her around and locked her up. She was only fourteen or fifteen herself then.

One does what one is doing because if one didn't want to do it one would obviously be doing something else. That's very popular psychological theory, now and then. Fear. Fear. A thousand ravens circling the eyes, their sharp beaks reflecting the sun. How many ways can he harm me? And if my parents do not care enough to come and get me out of this mess, then who will take care of me or care for me if I run away from Ross? Who will pay any attention?

Some of it dazzles, some of it flashes from the corner of the mirror, nevertheless . . . Peggy had a pair of black leather pants, just a little too tight and a vest that went with them, which hung between waist and thigh, leaving the front of her chest bare—tits playing hide and seek with the voyeur or lover (who is it, manufactures these things?).

Ross took a couple of belts from his closet. Thick ones, with brass buckles. He was blond too, and had green eyes. Nearly six feet tall and very solid. Peggy sat in the big wooden chair, laying her forearms carefully in the middle of the armrests. Ross wound the belts around her arms like bracelets and tightened them until she winced.

"I won't hurt you, Peggy, it's only a game."

"You'll stop if I ask you to?"

"Of course."

He had a long leather whip that ended in a tail of twelve lashes. One for each month, for each tribe of Israel, three for a season, this one might as well be winter, with snow two feet deep and drifting outside the house, the back lawn barricaded by walls, trees and shrub, far enough away so that no one could see it without binoculars.

Peggy was in the living room, tied to the chair. She could see the coffee stains from last week's spill. And the cigarette burns in the wood. Ross didn't mind the coffee spilling, or the tea leaves, but Peggy had a habit of leaving her Larks burning end up whenever she was finished with them, and letting them burn down to the filter—sometimes they would topple, and burn the furniture. WACK. Slap. "You stupid slut, how many times have I told you not to do that?"

Ross twirled the leather strips gently in Peggy's face. He brushed her hair back from her shoulders with them. He ran them down the length of her cleavage, to the small fat roll at the top of her pants (though Peggy, remember, weighs in at ninety-eight at the beginning of chapter seven—the pants were very tight). *(83)*

Wsssssssssssssh—SLAP!

Almost kindly on her small thighs. Leather hitting leather made a hot sharp noise—and a beginning of heat in her body, at the point of contact, a light, white circle sending small red arrows down her legs, into her groin.

Ssssssss. WHUP!

Harder. She wanted him to look at her, to make sure it was games they were playing, that she could do it next to him.

Wssssshhhhhhhh. Ssss. WHAP WHAP WHAP!

Her shoulders and sides began to burst with the heat and the circle was no longer white but red and she was not sure she liked this.

"Ross?"

"Cry, dammit, cry you bitch!" Is he crazy? Is this how it goes? Is this what men like? Look at me, Ross. Are you there? *Jesus he's insane.* There is *nothing* behind his eyes. *Ross, Ross.*

"Goddammit, Peggy! *Cry!*" The last lash hit her hand and drew a line of blood across the knuckles. She clenched her fist but she was too far away from him to give him what he was demanding, too afraid.

If only I could hurt you, if only I could make you feel me in a way you will never forget—joy is simple, fucking is simple, this power to torture each other, this, Peggy, *this*, is all that men have to leave their marks forever on each other's minds, woven into the cloth of will. I *must* hurt you, I *must* be given access to your pain, to your suffering, or I will never reach you, never love you, never trust you . . .

WHAMMMMM!!!!

He'd cut a long line down her chest and her left breast had started to blotch purple beneath the loose leather.

"You're crazy, you're crazy, you're crazy, let me go, let me go" . . . her eyes wide and her mouth open, drawing in huge gulps of air against the pain, shaking her head from side to side.

"Shut up! Shut up, you—pig! Cry, why don't you cry?" He slashed at her chest again and the whip came up dripping blood from seven of its tentacles. He dropped it and started to slap her face but she kept saying *you're crazy, you're crazy, you're crazy* in a monotone, without crying.

"*You're* the crazy one around here, you whore,

you can't cry! You're not human! You're not a woman!" He shook her shoulders and pushed the whole chair to the floor, where Peggy lay on her side, blood trickling into the blue pile rug, the belts cutting hard into her left arm.

Ross ran outside into the snow. He had no shirt on. His penis was stiff in his jeans. He unzipped them and pulled it out, with his knees sinking down a foot beneath the hard layer of ice from the last fall. He moaned very little until he came, clawing at his prick with his hands. Do you want it to be sunset? Probably it is only the middle of the afternoon. Around three. His come freezes a track along the snow. His hands drop and he bends his face into the cold white crystals, getting a little of his own seed on his forehead, then scouring it off with handfuls of snow—until he became aware that his whole torso was shaking convulsively from the cold (the cold?) and walked back inside.   (85)

°

"Did he untie you?"

"No, I was just lying there—I think I passed out after awhile—before he came back in, anyway. Because I didn't hear him come in, I only heard the shower running. That creep. He didn't even unbuckle me until he had finished taking a shower. I pretended I was still out. He said, 'Peg? Peggy? Hey, Peggy, answer me, c'mon, Peggy, are you okay?' Jesus, there I was strapped to the fucking chair and he was asking me whether I was okay and there was blood all over me and the rug. Very messy.

"Anyway, I just kind of grunted a little and opened an eye. I said, 'Get me out of here, please.' I think. I don't know what I said. I really hurt. Then he got down on his knees in front of me, and very quietly undid the belts and picked me out of the chair and took me to our bed.

"He got some alcohol and cotton and rubbed the cuts very gently. I was afraid, you know, he was going to start slapping me or rubbing real hard, to make the gashes bleed again, but he didn't do any of that, he was very quiet, and then he just sat there and watched me for awhile, not blank, you know, like before, but puzzled. I felt sorry for him. I don't know why but I felt that we had lost everything then, but not me so much, really, as him, you know, because he was already twenty-two, and he wanted something and all I knew about it was that emptiness—that total void behind his eyes and there was nothing I could do to understand what was happening in him.

"I must've fell asleep again because when I woke up he was naked and crouched next to me, under the blanket, in the fetal position, rubbing my breasts mechanically, and it hurt from the whip but anyway I put my hand on his head—my hand still hurt too, I remember, from where it was cut, on the knuckles. The knuckles bled a little for a couple of days.

"He got up and started making dinner. A friend of his came over and asked what was wrong with me, but Ross said it was nothing, I had my period, you know."

Peggy lit a cigarette from the one she was smoking and left the old one to burn out end up, on our night table.

"Men are so fucked up," I said.

"Some men, anyway. When I think about it now, I think I should have told him to enlist in the army," Peggy said. Abby and Inez are drifting out of her story and into making love.

"Anyway," she kept on, "they went out to a movie and the next day when Ross left he just locked the doors and said for me not to go anywhere and I didn't because—where would I go? I hurt too much anyway so I mostly lay in bed and read Ellery Queen . . ."

Abby is trying to tickle Inez's side with her feet, at the same time that Inez is handwrestling her and losing. Violence and torture were too far from them. They hadn't really heard the story.

Peggy wanders into the kitchen, which was her bedroom in that little Colorado apartment. She was getting lonely, then. There was nothing to do for it, she supposed, but start sleeping with Tim, the landlord's friend, just back from the Arctic and rooming downstairs.

The Committee of Investigation on Reliability and Narcotics Control makes a preliminary report on Inez Riverfingers:

Who does she think is going to believe this garbage? There were a few moments in the beginning where it seemed that this Inez Riverfingers was trying to make an honest attempt at a creative contribution, but we have lost all hope of that.

We have had very little luck in procuring character references of any substantial nature.

We have appended our interview with "Natasha Riverfingers" as proof of this, although it does lend some credibility to the smuggling fantasy in which our subject indulges.

At best, Inez Riverfingers appears to be a gifted but warped and isolated personality, bent on cashing in on the more sensational aspects of currently fashionable antisocial behavior. She lives and writes in solitude while engaging in spurious unAmerican activities, such as her connection with the Los Angeles Gay Liberation Front, which is under surveillance by the F.B.I.

Due to her incapacity to maintain any kind of close relationship at this point in her life, we feel that the probability of an actual hashish smuggling operation is very questionable. However, we feel constrained to recommend that no further action, such as hospitalization, be taken until we have cleared up the business of this narcotics fantasy to our own satisfaction. We are sure you will understand the necessity for precaution without further explanation.

Should we ascertain that there is no threat in terms of narcotics control, we will make recommendations for whatever treatment would be most likely to bring this girl back to a more social context. We can state at this time that it is our unanimous opinion that she should be prevented from any kind of independent, non-team work in the future.

We trust that all this remains, as usual, in the strictest confidence, for we are ever ready to admit possible error on our part, so long as such would create no breach of public trust.

Sincerely yours,
The Committee

Inez Riverfingers would like to make it perfectly clear that she is aware of the Committee's recommendation against her. And will continue to do as she is doing. There is a power afoot, to which certain parties seem totally oblivious. Their tough luck.

Furthermore, the question of truth in a narrative, whether or not that narrative claims to be directly related to the experiential, is a question best left either to those that write them or those who spend a great deal of their time ruminating over what it *is* that actually constitutes any given human experience.

Your notions of what "reality" is, gentlemen, seem based on a common error in the Western time sense: that there is in fact a past we can pinpoint, other than the shape our experience as a whole takes on in an immediate present, which itself drops from us continually, to the point where one would be hard pressed to take seriously any suggestions that the world has a precise and knowable form. I (89) do not suggest that I am writing a complex anti-linear tract—far from it. All I have ever said was that I was writing the pornographic novel of my life, for the sake of having something to do with my spare time.

Poor organisms that we are, we have little to set us free from the bonds of time, space and economics, save our own creative acts of will.

I hope this will give you gentlemen some pause in your rather hasty recommendations concerning my work and myself, both of which I love. Thank you for your attention to this matter.

The goddess in me salutes the goddesses in you,
Inez Riverfingers the First

P.S. You'll never get me anyway. I have more friends than even you can anticipate.

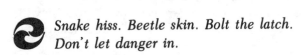 *Snake hiss. Beetle skin. Bolt the latch.
Don't let danger in.*

Abby had promised her mother she would take good care of Inez in Colorado. She tried. But it was all new to her. Inez had the advantage of having imagined it, although she had imagined it differently. She had imagined she would be able to talk at one a.m., to say everything in a rush, to be able to explain everything. Abby, however, had no experience at one a.m. listening. She was in fact a sound and early sleeper.

They wrestled for the focus. "Once upon a time there was a wonderful bear, named Lucy," Abby would say. Or, "No, Inez, I don't think we should go down to the university looking for acid. I think we should get more exercise, go for a walk in the mountains." And, "Yes, Inez, it's right, you're right, we should take this time and just enjoy it for what it is, but I can't help being anxious. You're going to college and you know what you're doing, but all I can do is take pictures, and I don't know what I'm going to do with my life."

Abby and Inez were seventeen. Inez was very sure of herself and had full faith in the fashions of her peers, with which she tried to indoctrinate Abby. See, we are just like every other teenage couple. Drugs, exclusive pairing, existentialism, the intellectual elite. And whatever you do, just don't leave me. I'll strain the dictionary for every ten syllable word that will keep you beside me. How will I ever like myself if, night after night, you don't console me?

In 1967 it was a disloyalty to doubt your lover. Abby and Inez were full of doubts they couldn't express. Later their silences, however innocent, would turn against them. Now the struggle was merely an occasional incident, only a shadow, easy to turn away from.

Besides, they were having a hell of a good time in bed. Reading the Tarot, they would draw the Lovers as the card of their outcome. They had the tremendous luck of being able to teach each other everything about their bodies from the beginning, with a little coaching from their friend, Peggy Warren.

"You can't tell me you didn't know *which* hole hid your hymen?" Peggy said. They would give her little smiles like crushed wads of paper laid out smooth again.

(91)

"I was afraid to sleep with you because I thought you would be so experienced," Abby told Inez. "It's hard to believe you're such a child. Come here, bum, don't give me those big sad eyes."

Peggy Warren would watch them, sighing. She spent her days soliciting contestants for Miss America in shopping malls. It paid okay. It certainly seemed to be less honest work than just about anything else she could think of. There's a certain discomfort one feels, going up to pretty women, saying, You look like a winner to me, baby—wanna try for the big time? Just then Peggy couldn't figure it out.

Soon Abby was going to follow Inez to college

and she, Peggy, was going to have to go back to Highland and finish school, or else go to public school in New York. She was a champ at talking, but not about how she was just sixteen and scared. No one really reached out to her except men who wanted a lay, and she let them if they were good-looking enough. She needed to be touched and there were no other ways of touch available. No one Peggy knew could talk about their real needs and feelings; she felt a big distance between herself and Abby and Inez.

Fortunately Inez and Peggy had managed to stop hating each other. Peggy saw that Inez was just another hungry kid. Inez realized that Peggy never was an ally of Allen's, she just slept with him. She had the start of an affection for Peggy, like yeast budding in cold water. They had come to tolerate each other: after all, they were both just women.

Abby was talking better, but she had no reason to reach for Peggy. Inez wouldn't have tolerated it. Inez needed her undivided concern almost as much as her cat, Kloop. Abby made Inez give up smoking Camels and all but a little dope. And Inez returned that concern as much as she was able. She opened to Abby's senses, let Abby show what she saw in animals and mountains, in the lens of her camera. Sight began to join them.

Still they were full of doubts they had no way to talk about. Partially because they were too engrossed in learning all the sexual alphabets, all the things no one had ever dared say out loud in their presence suddenly began to be whispered from their own mouths. They laughed when they read in the newspapers that there was more to marriages than sex. They boasted to each other about how many orgasms they had (although they weren't sure they knew what an orgasm was).

In men after all they come and you can see it, it's very specific. They were both positive they had orgasms, because of the way they breathed (the green breathing waves and all the other symptoms and waves they had) but no one, not even Peggy Warren, had ever told them what an orgasm was supposed to feel like. Sometimes they would have quiet ones, sometimes very noisy ones, and sometimes they felt that maybe they were making it all up.

Small breeze moves the curtains. In slow motion we undress, sink our unshaved kneecaps into the mattress. The breeze becomes a current, air turns wet, wind into water, miracle again! The river is over us and under us and I am on top of her, pushing down, pushing down with my pelvis, my breasts sweeping across her chest, and her hands locked into the skin on my back, and she is pushing up, with the same rhythm, the same breath, the same motion of fins gliding upstream. One wave, one rush, one which is us, the river everywhere, clear and fast, licking the pebbles of it, cold and fresh, our lips pressed together, our breasts joined like pyramids, their line in complete harmony, I push my stomach down into hers, which she is sucking in, and then she sighs her belly out, pushing mine in, springs creaking, turning over and she is on top of me, reaching down with her long fingers, rubbing the inside of my leg, then clitoris, then in me, one finger, two, three and I rattle in the bed, hair hanging off side, neck down, she's covering it

(93)

with kisses, I shift my weight sideways and she withdraws, wiping the white liquid on the side of the sheet—now I reach down into her folds, rubbing the clitoris in a circle, sucking her breasts—two, three, four fingers, slowly, carefully, like turning a cork in a bottle neck, the whole hand.

Completed, it was as if there were a golden hoop that looped through both our vaginas, hooped deep into our centers, the place of energy and creation in women, connecting in our stomachs flattened against each other all gold, all glowing

> A thousand atom angels—look!
> now I can count them—
> 　　　　　　　　　　dance
> on the hoop of our pin.

Rainbo Woman gets a higher education. Rainbo Woman dons raincoat, shuffles to classes. She is suspect. She remains silent. She will never be an astro-physicist, she will never graduate from college.

Last week I went to the Dean and asked him for a refund for my dorm room.

He said, "You know freshmen have to pay for dorm rooms. No exceptions, unless you're married."

I said, "I know. I've read the catalog." I said, "You see, I think I qualify. It seems to me and to the woman I live with, that we *are* married."

The dean turned a little red, sitting there in his carpeted office. He's known here as a good guy, a friend of undergraduates. He said, "Do your parents know about this?"   (97)

"Yes, sir."

"Do you have a roommate in the dorms?"

"Yes, sir. Her name is Eulalee. But we hardly ever see each other because I don't live there."

"Well, this is an unusual case," he said. "I'll have to consult my colleagues, and we'll let you know. Come back in a week."

Then he calls in Eulalee, to verify my story. She said he asked her, "Doesn't it bother you, that your roommate's a homosexual?"

"Why should it?" she said she said.

"Well, you're a very tolerant girl," he said.

It occurs to me that maybe I like this girl, Eulalee, even if she is a virgin. Someday we may even be friends.

So today, the dean recalled me. He cleared his throat a lot. He, too, goes to the movies.

"Inez," he said. "I've talked to a number of people about this, and we all think that to make an exception for you, although I do admit you have a good point, would call unnecessary attention to yourself, would make it more difficult for you to make the right—adjustment to college life. Do you see what I mean?"

"You mean," I said, trying calmly to hear him, watching the motorcycle I was going to buy with the dorm refund fade away, the one that would speed me through the gritty Portland rain. "You mean, people would wonder why you made an exception for me, and find out."

"Exactly," he said. "And we wouldn't want that to happen, would we? Now, what we can offer you instead is free psychiatric treatment—we have a special fund, for this kind of problem, and we'd be glad to make it available to you."

"I'll think about it," I said.

This is really what he said to me. When I am writing it here on this page I have a hard time believing it.

What would Rainbo Woman do in a situation like this? Use her silver bullets? What chaos, what turmoil—the term's oil, turn, oil us a piece. It's true, I can't understand anything. I can't even understand my classes. Maybe I am crazy.

Reed, March 17, 1968

It's harder and harder to write anything. Abby is confused by my writing now, though she tries to encourage me, and then I feel guilty when I'm not writing. It seems like all I want to do is lie in bed and have her hug me. It seems like it takes too much energy to make love anymore, and that frightens me. Everything frightens me. I can't stand going to classes anymore.

Abby wants to study photography, and I figure, she followed me to school one year, I can follow her one year, too. That way it'll take us eight years to get through college. Which is just as well—I can't think of anything else I know how to do, except go to school. So. I'm applying for a leave of absence, and we'll go wherever Abby gets in.

May 10, 1968   (99)

As soon as I pass my driver's test we'll start packing for Chicago. When I was a kid, I always wanted to live in Chicago. I think maybe because of Judy Garland. But every time I break into my famous Judy Garland imitation, Abby hits me on the head with a rolled up newspaper.

Cheeeecaygo, October 1968

Yesterday we got a letter from Peggy Warren, who's now a freshman at the University of Colorado. It was strange to get the letter.

I wish Peggy were here, so we could talk. Abby and me, we ain't talking real good at all anymore.

She's going to the movies with this skinny photographer/biker. Most of the time I just sit here. I can't ever seem to write. Every morning across the street an old man comes out of his apartment building with a folding chair and sits on the tiny square of grass, in front of the row of buildings. At sunset he goes in. I spend a lot of time watching him.

December 1968

Can't write, can you? Not good for much, are you, Inez? Well, at least you can get a job folding ladies' underwear in Korvettes, for two dollars an hour. It doesn't seem like knowing Greek is good for much. Natasha is going to have a baby. At least life goes on somewhere. Certainly there is no life folding underwear, folding imitation leather panties and leopard print slips. And all the time they are yelling at me to be interested in my work, to get into the inventory. Does most of the world do this? Suddenly it makes no sense at all that we haven't all risen in collective revolt, in disgust if nothing else, at the trap: women spending an hour in warehouses with muzak playing, trying to decide if they should get short or long, black bikini or the cute ones with the hearts all over them. I try not to look at them.

Meanwhile all the time, all the time Abby and this joker. Them going to the movies, them working in the darkroom, them going to parties, them sitting in our apartment making plans about bicycle shops. Now they are fucking. At this exact moment they are fucking, in my bed. I see my face reflected in the glass below the streetlamp. I can't stand it.

No. Wait. Think about it clearly. You Inez, you are the queer around here. Remember, Abby said she wasn't a lesbian, she only loved you.

Chicago, February 1969

Keeps on like the rawness of the wind. Last week I quit working at Korvettes. They wanted to fire me anyway, for not sorting bras fast enough. Another lackey bites the dust. This week, this week I have seen ten movies. Down at the Clark, where they hit you up with a double feature for seventy-five cents.

"Abby," I says, "do you really like sleeping with him? I mean, do you really like the sex, do you do cunnilingus and everything?" Yes, she says to me, yes, she does. "But, you bum, I still like you, I still like sleeping with you. Don't I always ask you to come back to bed with me after he leaves?" Yes, you do, Abby. Only the sheets smell of come.   *(101)*

April in Chicago 1969

It gives me a great sense of strength to see two women make love. Even if they are just Abby and Peggy.

Better around here for a few days since Peggy came and left. It was all very weird, but also exactly normal. She comes complete with crabs. Another twentieth-century disease. What's good about living in the city is that when your friends discover they have crabs you can get a bottle of A-200 at three a.m. Then it was perfectly natural to be rubbing it into her crotch. Her hair there is all blond and white, and I leaned my forehead against it, and that seemed to break a part of the barrier that was between us, me and Peggy, for so long.

"I was beginning to get in with all these people who were shooting heroin, and it's very beautiful stuff, Inez, very beautiful stuff, but I began to get scared about it, you know? So I'm dropping out of college for a while, going back to New York City, to think about what to do next. Wanna come?"

I am not ready yet. I am not ready to leave Abby. I watched how it was, Peggy and Abby making love for the first time, and I thought, maybe it's not real at all, this stuff I have been feeling and thinking and thinking and thinking about normal women, real women.

Peggy and me, we don't have much to say to each other with our bodies. It's nice, sleeping with her; comfortable. Maybe I don't have it together to be making love with anyone now. Does that happen to people sometimes? Am I frigid? I should leave Abby. I can't leave Abby. This is nonsense.

One morning, when she was here, Peggy woke and smiled at me in a way which made us very close to each other. I am not sure if it's clear, that a smile can be more than night after night of fucking hard and rubbing the old bones around in their circular pits. It surprises me some that it is, raised on the lap of holy mother orgasm as I've been. I suddenly feel like I don't understand anything. I'm not saying I don't understand just because I know it's a sign of humility to not understand, a backwards way of saying: boy, am I a groovy wise woman. I really have no idea, this time. I feel sexually inadequate, that's for sure, but that's all I know. I know Abby is

(102)

going to leave me. That's two things that I know. Which goes to show where knowing's at.

Also I know that the Indiana Tollway has these big signs on it, saying: *Welcome to the Main Street of the Midwest.* I know that because that's where we dropped off Peggy, on her way to the big time and the big city. Gonna struggle to be an actress.

We are all going to be famous. It's going to be Paris again and 1920. Famous! I can't even keep the little pot plants alive in the windowsill.

May

Now it is time. Should I stay and become a Chicago anarchist, a bomb in each bra cup? I am crying. I am a lonely kid in a Chicago apartment only two flights up, beating my fists against the side of my desk, crying.

Now all we do is fight. Well, we don't fight all the time. We just don't talk anymore. Two weeks ago I was coming home from the movies one night, for instance, and his car was still parked in front of the apartment. Abby promised he would be gone. I walked around the block eight times. Once a woman passed me and I saw her reach over and lock her car door, on the passenger's side. I must look deranged now.

I kicked his fender and bent his aerial. Finally I went inside. I wanted to get into my own bed. I was tired. I hate sleeping in the army cot in the living room. I made as much noise as I could, so they would know I was home, so Abby would send him back to mom and dad on the other side of town.

And all this time I've gone along with it, all this

(103)

time she's said, "But if I told him about you and me, it would *kill* him. I know it would." Deception after deception—the loyal roommate.

I was making all this noise. But he didn't come out. So I started in again, talking to myself, making whatever noises I could make that weren't screaming. That weren't saying, goddammit get your ass out of my bed I want to go to sleep now.

Then I heard him talking. He was making jokes about me. He was making fun of me to her. I could only hear phrases out of what he said. But I heard her laughing at them. I heard her laughing with him at me so that he wouldn't know she was a queer too. I heard Abby laughing at me.

Guess I'll go to New York for awhile, and hang out with Peggy.

May End

(104)

We were going to drive across together, me and Abby, from here to New York. For old times' sake. I remember, I have to remember.

We can't drive to New York now. Something— the timer, I think, broke on the car last night, and Abby came back here and said, "You know how you always tell me I should take things more as a joke and be more existential?"

"Yes," I said, though now it seems a little ironic that it's me who says it.

"Well, the car broke down and I sold it to this guy who was standing there for twenty-five dollars."

"Twenty-five dollars!" I exclaim. "Goddammit,

Abby, we put more than nine hundred dollars into that thing!"

"But Inez, don't you think it was existential?"

"It was existential, all right."

She was right about that, anyway. It was very existential. So I write home for bus fare to New York, and we divide up our things. You can have the Stones albums if I can have the Beatles.

New York City, August 1969

This morning I kissed Abby goodbye when she got on the plane for Israel (but on the cheek, her parents were watching). Just as if it were 1942, the trains leaving the stations in Paris, and Humphrey Bogart disappearing into the mist. We look into each other's eyes and it's there—an instant when it seems all possible again. Part of me is very glad to see her go. Now I can try to be Inez again, instead of a conglomerate. What I miss most is her presence. I read that somewhere, when you stop living with someone what you miss is their presence. Another grade B cliche accomplished and gone. (105)

Yesterday I got a letter from Natasha (I am writing this at my grandmother's apartment. Grandma's in California) which I'll copy here, since I feel like writing but everything sounds like mush.

Do you think it's a fantasy to think you have a destiny? That in some ways your life is all laid out in front of you and you're just pulled along the track and oh yes *you* may stop at a few stations that might not have been on the route, but it's mostly all there and you knew the way all along... or are some people witches, and exempt, and able to make up their own lives? I wonder this a lot tonight, Inny, sitting up a little tipsy and staring at newsprint vanishing in the fire...

N.Y.C. September 13, 1969

We pick up the habit, from all these years going to school, of needing to go somewhere when it's August and September. Peggy and her latest boyfriend Bruce are going to Europe tomorrow. I myself, for no better reason than to take some courses at an art school, am going to Los Angeles next week. No one in their right mind goes to Los Angeles, so that proves I'm crazy, once and for all. But my grandmother's coming back, and I can't face looking for an apartment in New York.

Dear Grandmother, would that you knew what has happened in your apartment while you've been gone. Certainly it would be more titillating than "The Secret Storm" or the biography of Napoleon I found on your night table. Let me tell you this once, Grandma, and don't worry about it, it's only how you say? a difference in generations:

Three days ago I was lonely, Grandma. (Grandma, you remember that nice Jewish girl who was my roommate, Abby? She did what nice Jewish girls do, she went to live on a kibbutz. Would it surprise you to know, Grandma? Maybe not.) I went looking for my friend, Peggy, who's been working as a photographer's model, making good money, making twenty-five dollars an hour, so she could go to Europe. My favorite picture is the one they made of her under the caption: "I was my Husband's Mistress' Lover," which showed her and another girl nude except for black lace stockings and high heels, sitting on a fur-covered bed, in full color, their legs interlocked so as to show their vaginas (they call that spreadshots, Grandma), their arms interlocked so that they were licking each other's big purple popsicles.

I found my friend Peggy, along with her boyfriend, a nice boy she met at college, name of Bruce, her sister and her sister's boyfriend, hanging around at Peggy's mom's, watching t.v. I persuaded them to come over here, where it would be more private. So all five us came back here, to talk, amid your mid-Victorian furniture. (Grandma, did you ever sit naked on those tapestry-bottomed antique chairs?)

The most memorable thing about this particular   (107)
evening is how fucking hot it was—at least a hundred—and as soon as we got here, Peggy and Bruce stripped, and, following their lead, I took off everything except a business shirt I ripped off from my dad years ago. I'm not *that* used to being uninhibited around strangers. Peggy's sister and the boyfriend, Phil, I think his name was, were a little nervous and very much wanted to be hip.

You can see it: all sitting around in those scratchy tapestry chairs, amidst china vases and beaded bell pulls, in an apartment that smells like chicken soup, some naked and some dressed. Bruce was mainly involved in trying to tell Phil that bisexuality is a common, an even basic, trait in the human species.

That is, he wanted to lay Phil. Since Peggy's sister seemed to be the first woman this Phil character had ever slept with, he wasn't sure he even liked straight sex, and got very uptight about Bruce's manipulations. I started to mumble to myself about men, and raided your liquor cabinet.

We drank for awhile, and we smoked some dope, and it began getting very late, like, two a.m.—so I rolled out the hydabed from beneath my great great grandpa's oil portrait. I winked at him. I said: Great great Grandfather, I know you were a happy little capitalist, making a fortune in cigars, and I hope that in life you were also a letcher and voyeur, because if you were, tonight's your night. Which it was.

I didn't know a hydabed could hold so many twisting people or positions! Most of the time it was impossible to tell who it was groping you or whom you were groping. But it got so it didn't matter, everything felt good. Bruce and I made love for a while, even. He came in me, and I was pleased because Peggy says he has a hard time coming. I felt a little better, knowing I could satisfy someone.

Around four a.m. Bruce had begun to get it on with Phil, and I was wearying some of the old body-roll in the heat, even though Bruce kept saying "the hotter the better" because he comes from the tropics or something (I have stopped wondering where Peggy finds these people). He's leaving with Peggy tomorrow for Europe, so she must like him. She says he shoots a lot of heroin, but maybe it will be different in Europe, better for them—or else they'll split up. We had to get butter from the refrigerator to cool off their pricks, Grandma, because we couldn't find where you stashed your vaseline. It was interesting, to watch them butt-fucking, but it seemed kind of distant to me, all I could do was make terrible jokes about hot-buttered balls.

Then Peggy and I decided we'd split from the general *melee*, and we went to sleep in your room. Bruce and Phil and the sister kept chugging for at least another hour and a half, because I remember opening my eyes in the first dawn, hearing a little very awake scream from the other room, seeing Peggy smiling in her sleep, in my arms, and nodding back out myself.

I don't mean to be so cynical with you, old lady. I love you very much. Certainly you were always closer and kinder to me than my own mother. I don't know how to get across all these distances very well yet, though. It seems like the older I get, the more distances there are. Real ones in space, real ones in my mind. I don't think it will be any better in Los Angeles, but at least it's a different place. I know it confuses you, Grandma, that I move around so much, you who've lived in this one apartment for twenty years now, for as long as I can remember.

For some the garden, for some the journey, is home. You know what I mean? The other day I was walking in Central Park, and I saw a row of old ladies eating ice-cream pops with white goves on, in the tremendous heat. And I realized that I might be the only person to ever have that experience, watching old ladies eat ice cream with their gloves on, or I might be one of millions, but that my experience of it was totally private.

For twenty years now you've had the courage to be alone in this apartment. I respect that courage, even if I take such outrageous advantage of your absence. I am alone now with my memories of orgies and of Abby in Colorado. I am alone with what happened to me in Chicago. I am alone with Rainbo Woman. I am alone with the sight of old ladies eating ice cream with their clean white gloves on. It's a little frightening, but we all have to come to it. You manage, after all, with the afternoon soap operas and your biographies of Napoleon.

(110)   Disown them as she may try, Mr. & Mrs. Bramanoi and their youngest child, Albert (rechristened Al Bear Riverfingers by Inez, ten years his senior), write a few words to their only daughter as she travels. They love her, they try to love her, they try anyway to give her a sense that she has a family background.

August, 1963

Dear Inez,
    Albert is now going to type a few words to you all by himself.
    sally runs tothe car.Dick play ball.
    Thank uyou very much for therecord. Itis a
    nice record.I love ey you   very much.
    Jane fell down.Spot bit Puff.

Albert

May, 1964

Dearest daughter,

It was so good speaking to you on the phone. Things here follow their usual course. Mommy is usually in pain but bears up well. And I go on working. Now that I have given up psychiatry, I am lost. Instead of weird dreams, I have nightmares. No one ever knows the private hells that exist in the minds of others or the loneliness. When I had my kidney stone all I could think about besides the pain was you and how awful it would have been if this happened when I was alone. I started to worry about your being alone. I am concerned that man because of his frailty and lack of physical ability to cope with his environment is a gregarious animal. He *needs* people to help him live. We all live needing other people. Enough philosophy. How's kicks? Can't wait to see you. All my love,

Daddy

June, 1966

Dear Inez,

I love you very much. School is very good and my report card is best and I got all A's and B's, too. I'm doing very good in school but school is out now and we have a summer vacation. School is out, play begun.

Mike just had his birthday party and he's 11 years old and he had a picture of two bats and a ball on his cake. I'm doing very good in my swimming. I went to the beach yesterday and Mike got a fishing rod for his birthday from his dad and I gave him Flubber but that was nothing much. I think that's all.

Love,
Albert

Dear Inez,

I only wish I could express myself as well as you do, could put thoughts and feelings on paper in the magic, meaningful ways you do. I'm slowly getting back to my typewriter (your father insists I should write more) but still the mechanical instrument fights back. But I shall try to tell you what reactions your letter brought, what latent feeling and emotions within me.

First of all, your letter about you and Abby clarified, in a way, what I was mulling over in my heart and mind these past months and I tried to express to you during your visit here spring vacation: all of us here love you very much—if a child does well she should be happy and of course mother and father will be at ease. But, as your mother, perhaps greatly aided by five years of my own psychiatry and gaining more insight thereby, I came to realize that I have always loved you (fat, thin, bright, stupid, responsive, withdrawn, etc.) and I don't even know exactly if it's because you are my daughter, though I know it may be trite to repeat the old cliches of "mother's love is a birthright" and "even a beetle is beautiful in the eyes of its mother." I say these things to you now for several reasons: perhaps I myself have been too "hung up" to express them before to you and you have been out of the family environment for so long that you cannot really know that you would have actually felt this love constantly had you lived with all of us, even in the midst of fights, yellings, scenes, worries and problems.

Your relationship with Abby, as you described it so well, comes as no great shock or surprise to me or would to those who have known you best through these years. I know that you have been kind of wavering back and forth about homosexuality for a long time (forgive my nonscientific language) and

(112)

that was evident often from other graspings for relationships you had; that whatever you feel you must do to maintain your happiness and dispel the fears that go bump in the night can only bring happiness to me, too . . . I have long since learned that all is not black or white and mine is not to "approve" or "disapprove" but just try to understand and accept—this I do, in all good spirit and love (should add that, in my role of mother and omnivorous reader, I shall continue to caution against anything but brief, limited, experimental activities involving "mind-blowing" drugs and the like, including traveling around without using extreme caution and sense, which I think you have developed better than most—not that my cautions will prevent anything but it makes me feel better that I haven't been entirely remiss in "parental advice").

As for Abby herself, she did immediately strike me as a warm, sensitive, yearning person, the kind I instinctively like and want to be with, and I'm very glad now that you gave us the opportunity to meet her at your graduation. I wonder, not actually knowing them personally, if her parents are not aware somehow of your situation, if only subconsciously, and of course, most parents do not want to recognize any "divergencies" unless directly confronted. At any rate, I hope, for both of you, that your relationship is as warm and good as you make it sound.

You asked me to accept your life and you for what it is and you are. This you can count on always. We are here to be counted on and to be of help and to love you.

But also, there will be times when neither I nor your old friends will be available to you in Portland. I have mulled this over and feel it is fair enough to ask, in return for my understanding (not for my love—that is not on the "bargain" table), you

(113)

contact, at the *very first* opportunity when you get to Portland, a "good" psychiatrist, and try to make a start at regular appointments with him (or her)—believe me, Inez dear, this suggestion is not made because I have any notions that you are "sick" or that your relationship with Abby is "evil" or "unhealthy"—I just feel that there will be times, certainly, when you will need absolutely someone with whom you can talk and work things out.

I have never known many women—or men, for that matter—who were homosexuals, perhaps there were some who never "let it out," but it will be difficult, I imagine, for you to adjust to college life with this extra facet, and I want to make sure you can get whatever help you might need.

Daddy had not been feeling well for a couple of weeks and he desperately needs some rest. Frankly, Inez, I don't really know how *he* was hit emotionally by your letter because he doesn't talk much about these things (I used to think it was just him who was so reticent, but I am beginning to feel most men don't have the same facility for talking about their emotions as women do; that's nature, I guess). But you are his love—that you know without my rhetoric.

My arm is dropping off! Write (or rite, as Albert says)! All my love,

Mother

(114)

January, 1968

Dearest Inez,

I realize that it has been too long since my last letter (I can plead work, of which there is always so much I don't know what to do) or my own father's death, but these things are my worries—and you are my joy. Possibly that's why I have not written in so long—the Puritan in me keeps me from those I most enjoy.

But you worry me sometimes too. I never

answered/responded to your summer letter about you and Abby partially because I thought Mommy did such a good job and partially because I did not then, nor now, know what it is I should say, or want to say.

In some sense there is a parental feeling of failure—I know that is a social hang-up but it exists. The only homosexuals I ever knew were when I was in college, they were all men and seemed to me caught up in a trap of self-centered, egotistical (and brief) relationships to each other and the world, characterized chiefly by their vanity. I certainly hope that you will not become like that and I realize that these were only what they call the visible homosexuals. As I have always told you, I only want that you should be happy; if this is how you want to live your life, I accept it so long as it does not hurt you or anyone else and does not hold back or freeze your capacity as a productive person.

More than that I don't know what to say. I hope you are enjoying school and not working as hard as I have to, to keep you there. Seriously, I know the   *(115)*
competition is rough, but I'm sure you're doing well. You're my daughter, after all. I miss you all the time and wish you were here. You'll always be the girl of my dreams.

Love,
Daddy

Mom, I'm Glad You're Not a Scorpio

A mother is a strange object in my mind, one who scrapes out the lining of my intestines with a furcovered fork, whom I would please, whom I would be patient for, through the time when the question is asked and considered: When will you admit to knowing something about me? But there was never anything—a space you tried to cover with the cards of your boredom (boredom?).

mother
I have no comfort to give you, only shame.
Mother, so many impossible gestures built into the
blood because I can say to you, "I love you, I am
trying to" and you can tell me that a mother always
loves its child; but the lioness in the wood and
the bear by the stream full of their appetites love
nothing but themselves, with a tedious and lum-
bering instinct, and not with the knowledge of what
it is to die and what precautions must be taken in
the human state to keep the children of knowledge
from going crazy, wandering the earth in small
bands waking in the night for fear of noises and
afraid of the water and the sky. It takes more than a
blind rat gnawing at the trap door to tap the hidden
spring of what people can do for each other.
    mother
    This is a letter from me to you which I didn't
start out at. The Investigating Committee has my
name now because I joined the L.A. G.L.F. not to
mention Gay Women's Liberation in San Francisco
and other things I can't tell you about. They are
afraid because we are no longer separating out our
private lives from our public lives and they use
always the tools of the liberals to lobotomize the
revolutionaries. To be a lesbian is to be implicitly
revolutionary and I am just beginning to find out
what that means and so the slick men question and
where they can they jail or hospitalize. I'm not
making this up, mother, I've seen it.
    Mother, I am not sure where I am. I think I am in
love again but sometimes it slips from me while I
am out walking after sundown and I look at the
stars and feel as if no one will ever look up and see
me. The distances are too great, the buildings are
too long. There is a certain span where one hopes
and after that time of being able to hope one must
give in to being disappointed. One cannot reach in
voids every day, day after day, when day after day

the silver fish that flashes in the bright waters,
which our fingers touch, is gone. She does not hear
and I walk sometimes, over my body a kind of ache
after which the time of hope is gone. The pain,
once one has shrugged finally and said "I hear
nothing either," remains a kind of bitterness, a
tearing hunger, final impoverishment, and that is
what comes to me sometimes though I am still
hoping as yet and not really preparing for rejection.
But I am afraid and if I am going to be hurt again a
year since Abby's going I want it to be simple,
clean, anesthetic
    mother
    what could I teach you but how to look gently
beyond your own sorrow and fear into how human
that is, and how to move past our terrible isolation.
My dreams are of you by the sea and large buildings and elevators and the impossibility of it all,
about misunderstandings and betrayals and fleeing
and not being able to find the right apartment and
lost in the alarm clock lost in the work.
    mother   (117)
    these things granted: that you will never speak to
me and will never listen to my voice or the stories I
mean to tell you and the understanding and the
shield, the refuge, sanctuary, will never be given
me, nor clemency—you will not know what I mean
because you will answer "well, you have a way with
words" and gradually the letters will drift back to
being about how well you did in the last tennis
tournament and my letters will be about nothing.
With all of that it is enough you are a Sagittarius and
not Scorpio because the women with their black
hair, their fresh-bread-smelling breasts and their
spider-lady eyes are almost always those (inter-
twined with the gentle Tauruses who come to
rescue me when it becomes too hard). With the
Scorpio women it is always life or death (but
mother understand I have been hurt so by women

because I am an intense asking person. I am always asking and if they had been men instead it would have been much much worse. What I am saying is do not harbor a reserve, a pity, because what a shame it is that she can't be making these motions with the opposite sex. If it had been Scorpio men, mother, I would be dead). And if you had been, had had that hooked jaw behind the careless breath, the accidental brushing of hips at dinner and the denial always of your intentions I would have been mad long past. It is well you are a Sagittarius and tried to do your best and although nothing came of it at least it is not rape itself having to be faced each time you march across my memory, but only the sense of loss, a certain kind of long moon sadness, a fading Japanese print of it, with the sun going down and its red beams like searchlights over the highways

mother open this letter
I cannot bring myself to write it

(118)

    Naomi Riverfingers turned to Inez in the Gay Liberation office and hugged her, having read this letter. Naomi had only come to see how Inez was, to talk about a project Inez was planning, in Tangier. Naomi was not altogether comfortable in the Gay Liberation office; it was just to see Inez that she had come. They would sit and talk together, Naomi and Inez, about writing and revolutions, how the world is changing. Naomi liked the idea of strong women coming together to make a women's revolution. She liked it as an idea she might want to put into a dance. Naomi quickly saw that there were not many women in the Gay Liberation Front office. Inez was slowly coming to the same conclusion.

Naomi was seventeen, she was a dancer, and she lived with men. She had violet eyes and long black hair. They heard things about a women's movement, but for Naomi it would mean reconsidering the men. She wasn't ready. To Inez it meant calling Naomi her sister, which wasn't true. Naomi was a friend who had a strong taste for adventure. For Naomi knowing Inez was an experiment.

"I'm sorry. I can't," Naomi said after she read the letter. Naomi was not a Scorpio, but she knew she would do as well; she did not mean to get entangled in the part that was not an adventure, in the part that is about: will we be working for a good common life? She hugged Inez, and walked out. They would meet next week.

Inez folded the letter carefully into her notebook. Inez watched from the window, Naomi and her hair walking down the street.

(119)

An interlude. Naomi Riverfingers (who invented the name) writes Inez two letters, typical of the Southern California School. Typical, that is, of young girls with violet eyes, happy in the trouser summers.

Letter from One Waterbaby to Another

Let us just say we were born on the tide.
For a while I thought I was evaporated
rose water.

Inez Riverfingers said, "Pull the doves
from your pockets."
I remembered the wonderful apple dream.

Afterword

To all Russian sailors:
Remember your birthright. If you get
lost at sea,
think of a spring bubbling where brook begins.
Always keep a set of wings on hand for those
times when you want to fly away.
Remember to use your fins, you will be
surprised at the tricks they can help you do.

Dearead Rivfinnygerel,
     I used to have an overgrown starfish named
Harriet whom I fed matzoh meal and kept in a jar.
I was reminded, however passingly, of Harriet on
reading your letter which mentioned something
about your truck looking like a pubescent station
wagon bursting its britches, I just thought I'd
mention Harriet.
     About my official standing, I can't make a deci-
sion so I am sending you some lists of birds' eggs
and fish for comfort and inspiration.
     I have never seen a chicken's egg from the inside.
     The news from me is quagmire with an occa-
sional soft sunbeam and many invisible ones,
getting stronger I think. *I* will never call your
dreams an imposition. You know what I mean.

                    liters of letters, love, the Liquid Lady,
                              Naomi Riverfingers

P.S. If all else fails, you can call your new truck
Harriet.

This is still America, baby, and don't you forget it

It is not as if we have forgotten it. In 1969, for instance, a boy Inez and Abby had known in Portland, Oregon, had his head bashed in while standing in front of a medical tent they were defending in memory of the slain Kent State students. The citizens of Portland were not aware that their police force even had a Tactical Squad until that moment.

There is self immolation. In Chicago Inez and Abby begin the years of marching. Women in heels stand in front of the troop trains. Women have made a movie called "You Don't Have to Buy War, Mrs. Jones."

Inez and Abby do not own a television set. Everytime they accidentally see the six o'clock news Inez starts going to demonstrations again. Right there is the killing. And the commercials, in between the killings. The con that it is not happening. Certainly it is not happening to you.

(121)

Grandma:	King Xalta says the tree holds the wealth and history of his people?
Dondi:	So what's important about that?
Grandma:	I—I'm curious to know if his Anca people are really the Ancient INCA—or is King Xalta merely obsessed with a myth? After all, it is one thing to be an Inca Queen and quite another to be simply the wife of an aborigine.
Dondi:	But Gee, Grandma, if you LOVE King Xalta, what's the difference?

Grandma: I intend to take King Xalta back to New York with me and Taboo or no taboo—I MUST KNOW THE SECRET OF THE TREE OF KNOWLEDGE!

"Dondi," *The New York Post*, June 27, 1971

The Gay Liberation Front is a radical and revolutionary organization, based on anarchist guidelines, similar to the Black Panthers and Weathermen. The organization is worth watching, although there seem to be only one or two radical individuals present at any given time. There is no immediate threat. They represent themselves as a homophile organization, but are unlike such respectable and dedicated organizations as Daughters of Bilitis and Mattachine.

New York police report on the New York Gay Liberation Front, from *Gay Sunshine*, August, 1970

(122)

Los Angeles Times, in 1969, ran an article about computer poetry. The IBM 7094-7040 DCS was fed simple grammar, assorted stanzaic patterns, and a vocabulary of 950 words. One of the things it came up with:

Tremble like a red locomotive!
Flop like a damp gate!
The roses are vomiting.

Old Ammunition disposed of for North St. man.
Door Open at Whaconah Regional High.
State Police reported pieces of metal falling from sky near Dalton-Windsor line. Checked but found nothing.
Loud Music complained of. Took care of it.

"Dalton Police Log," June 22, *The Dalton News-Record*, July 1, 1971, Dalton, Mass.

Speaking to GAY's reporter in February, 1970, Dr. Leary gave his support to Gay Rights, adding that his friend, Allen Ginsberg, had opened his eyes to the plight of the homosexual as well as to his humanity. "Ginsburg," said Leary, "made it all come true for me . . . he is really an eloquent man, honest poet, and beautiful person." Dr. Leary continued: "It's about time the most articulate, sensitive, literary, wise and holy homosexuals give us the perspective of the homosexual trip."

Gay, New York City.

Why perverted people such as homosexuals of either sex should be allowed to flaunt their immorality and their abnormalities before the eyes and ears of decent people is something this newspaper does not understand. Presumably Police Authorities in . . . Bridgeport . . . feel they are under an obligation as a result of Supreme Court decisions to allow this type of filth to parade. But to this newspaper it makes absolutely no sense whatsoever.

(123)

The freedoms guaranteed by our Constitution were designed to create the freest expression and exchange of ideas; they were not designed to permit the public display of obscenity, smut and filthy ideas of any variety. In the same way we do not think the founding fathers ever believed that the guarantees given under the constitution for freedom of assembly would be used to propagandize and advertise abnormal and unnatural human behavior.

Editorial by Publisher Loeb,
Connecticut Sunday Herald, Father's Day 1971.

When asked the reason for his belated return to the arena, Luis Miguel says, "I am coming back in search

of an illusion, which to me is just as much as saying I
am coming to find complete happiness."

From an article about Picasso and his friends,
Los Angeles Times, 1971.

"Women who don't care about fashion distractions
are about as exciting as a glass of water," says Alice
Regensburg, American Footwear Institute executive.
[On the same page:]
Women get more headaches than men, or, to be
scientifically accurate, they at least are more likely to
use headache remedies than men, and to use them
more often.

"Women's Pages," *The Boston Globe*, 1973.

Bombs are falling while you are reading this. Do
not be frightened. Do not lose faith.

(124)

Peggy Warren corresponds from Europe
and the tip of Africa:

October, England
Dear Inez
Hope this finds you where it is you have disappeared. Anyway we got to London the next
night—as we pass through customs I turn and see
Bruce being stopped and held back, which gave me
visions of going off to London etc. by myself after
all (that 'after all' being that the morning after I last
saw you, Inny, Bruce and I split up and I thought I
was going by myself because of all the heroin Bruce

was doing and his being more turned on to guys than to me, besides wanting to pimp for me in the city—which we did once on the road which I never told you—in a greasy diner with some truck driver putting his arm around me—the bicep, I remember, was tatooed "MEG"—and him slipping Bruce ten dollars and then we had this huge meal and blew it all) anyway it was only that last time he was here he overstayed his visa and they wanted to scare him about leaving on time this time—but I nearly had a heart attack.

/I stopped because Bruce woke up and announced we were going to Dublin —I'm writing this from a 24 hr. cafe on the road. Anyway, to continue about London—Bruce got through—we went to Victoria station and tried to get the numbers of these people Ratato gave us— well, dearie, no good, because there are no telephone books for the whole of London, just parts— but meanwhile as I was phoning I laid down my little change purse with $90 and six pounds and lo and behold I turned around and it was gone—so much for $100, definitely stolen. We wandered around London for awhile looking desperately for a place to stay—about 3 a.m. around picadilly we ran into some London hippies who said sure mates and took us to a subway (cultural note: subway—definition: underground walk for pedestrians; "The underground" is the subway)—well it was about the same quality as in n.y. subways but cleaner— slept till 11 when people started walking by—it was raining. Thought about staying in London but Bruce decided that to travel was better but he kept changing his mind—which was starting to drive me crazy—finally we went—started hitching—which is legal thank god and here we are watching some wrestling and hoping to catch an all night ride from the Lorry drivers—

Well so much for our myriad adventures—

everybody write us care of American Express London—Inez there are so many things to say to you that I tried to get Ratato and Abby to express from me and Bruce that I just wanted to have you see—mainly about how much we love you and you really should live with us here or something (now Bruce is talking about going to the U. of Ireland because Dublin's very cheap) Bruce as you've gathered by now is quite erratic when it comes to deciding what he's doing/ Short pause—now it's Thursday—we got a ride and finally slept in a barn—had some problems with a truck driver who tried to cop a feel as we got out—Bruce says blue jeans are very non-respectable here and they think I'm a real bum—I refuse to wear a dress hitching— damn it the idea of traveling around like this is comfort—and who is comfortable in a dress? Things are sticky—I think it is just that I look like a whore no matter where I am—I always have trouble—in an evening gown I look cheap— blahhhh! I feel down—but I shan't always— remember about keeping in touch, my love

(126)

                              Peggy

                          month? year?
Inez dear

This letter coming as it does out of the tomb or in other words from the vast dark silence which has surrounded me, myself, and others such as Bruce, is to you—self-evident—onward—I am as the envelope suggests in Tangier wallowing in strange smoking materials—cheap, plentiful—no tars or nicotine—and letters are difficult to start, finish, send—not to mention finding IDH 10 for a stamp —which is   24 and buys 6 eggs, 200 gr. sugar or 3 eggs 1 kilo turnips and 3 cakes—therefore rendering stamps and communications low on the priority list. Bruce and I actually have written both

on paper and in our (mine at least) minds many
letters, expressions of thoughts, even facts; information—yes—item: Peggy and Bruce went to Paris
—Peggy worked in Paris hmmm that means
worked the streets with Bruce ever faithful bar-
tering my ass on the side—also begged in Paris,
took Acid in Paris, fixed heroin in Paris, bought
truck in Paris, split autumn in Paris leaving or being
asked to leave Bruce as somehow somewhere it
didn't work and I doubt we will ever see each other
again as one of us will probably die first—unless of
course he shows up here next month as he promised—end of sentence.

New Items—hitchhiked to Tangier in December
—had pack including camera stolen—bad—very
bad—finally in Tangier with a whole crew of
assorted freaks and madmen—living here a month
—broke but living somehow—strange how far the
States are—strange how far Bruce is—how far Inez
is—Abby is—and Peggy is in Morocco, stranger
still

(127)

March

I wrote the above while stoned—sphew!
awhile ago, after reading one of your letters. Just
got a letter from Abby written about a month or so
ago and have just written her. I sometimes think I
will go join her in Israel but I know I am not cut out
for the pure life, making the desert grow and all
that. Been here over 3 months with no money
which is really strange—I've been taking lots of
drugs—kief and hash are cheaper than food—as a
matter of fact we almost never pay for hash. But
speaking of that, if you want some, I'll send you
some—maybe we could do a whole operation? And
get me back to the beautiful U.S.A. where I can get
away (do I want to?) from all this morphine etc.
Just send me some money——I know what you are

probably thinking about trusting me but trust me anyway. We'll get up a great hash collective and bring in 9 kilo's strapped to my stomach or something.

Anyway here I am in Tangier with 2 cats on my lap. Sometimes I get letters from (of all people) Allen—remember him? and other old lovers—it all seems so far away. There's a charcoal fire in front of me, a guy named Bruce—whoops, you know Bruce, he reappeared out of the dust last month, smoking a sipsl (pipe of hash) and Muhammed & Jean are out trying to borrow money to eat and maybe fix drugs and it's Ramadan so nobody eats, smokes, drinks or fucks till 5:20 p.m. for a month which puts them all really uptight but when the cannon goes off everybody has Ramadan soup and stays up all night so as to sleep late—

Tangier is really a trip. How are you doing? If you can't get together the money for Superdeal come to Tangier—come to Tangier—come to Tangier—this is a spell I am trying to work as I am (128) so into potions of various sorts these days—dying for news—Are you in love? Are you sitting in some Los Angeles gay bar looking at legs (remind me to tell you about my latest theory, which is that heterosexuality is what's unnatural, next time I see you). What do you think about Abby doing Transcendental Meditation now? Are you happy, crazy, stoned, dead? I'm reading a book on zen macrobiotics and waiting for Muhammed to come back with eatables or shootables   Love, Peggy

Los Angeles, April, 1970

Dear Peggy,
Hope this letter isn't too late one way or the other. I am sick of L.A. and sick of sitting in my abandoned sunday school and writing and playing games with virginal teenagers and hanging out

down on Melrose where the gay bars are and never knowing what the hell is going on in my head or body. Thumpety thumpety. So—I am organizing with my savings and some friends (very few) a way of getting you some money so you can *really* smuggle seven kilos or more of hash into the uunyteed statez. We can send you $3000+ (+ for your plane fare, new clothes as I assume you look a little ragged and a false bottomed suitcase or whatever you choose) then you can come out to the great West Coast and we can sell dope and travel around America together in my International and look poor but always eat well and leave hundred dollar bills under poor people's plates and Christmas dinners for the families on relief.

I don't really believe in it, you know, as a way of life, so to speak, but it was either this or going back to work at Korvettes, which is *impossible*. When Abby comes back then we can all retire to the woods of Colorado or Oregon or Canada and build an octagonal cabin and live happily ever after——I'm serious.   (129)

Peggy. Can you be trusted? Has all that hash gone to your brain? Do you want to spend the rest of your life smoking (shooting) dope in Tangier? I could pucker my eyebrows and say a few very sensitive things about how I *know* you are not really happy and what a grungy scene it must be though necessary because everyone has to go through That Kind Of Thing Once but jesus Peggy you are only twenty, you know. America may be going down the drain fast (and Inez Riverfingers, your local lunatic, may be no one to speak) well perhaps I will put it this way—I miss you and need you to come back, this seems as good a way as any to get you here. I can't ever ask Abby to come back you know because that's not the way it is between us—so now it's time for a whole new set of Games.

It's not even that I am disenchanted with the

natural life (I wonder why I am spending so much time justifying this?). In a lot of ways I think Gay Liberation saved me (you too can be saved, yesss sirrr, just fill in this handy coupon folks, mail it today!) but G.L. should have come out about five years earlier (and I keep wondering, where are the women in it? and I can't get into any of the women I've met so far in the Women's Movement—they're all—I don't know how to say it exactly, they are very much caught up in trying to show that they're *women* whatever that means—anyway, even a baby butch like yours truly seems to put them up tight). Day by day I swing across the saw-toothed limbo—which world do I belong in, with what people? Gay bars, city artists, hideouts, meetings, antiwar rallies, SDS, country communes? I don't know. I want therefore this other thing—a time at least for head clearing, building up a little cash reserve, wandering around the country with you and living dangerously. Are you up for it? What do you think out there, Peggy?

(130)   I have come to the end of my own aereogramme. Let me know as soon as possible. Shantih, your ever faithful Inez Riverfingers

early may

Inez—Bruce died yesterday. Some other time about that. Too early for thinking. So I have got the hash in hand—Ahmed's best and I've been here long enough to know. He only wanted to give me seven keys for the money but I held out for nine, which I told him was a luckier number in America and he didn't want me to go without Yankee luck—actually, I balled him is why we got such a good price and the extra key and all—ugh. Anyway I am going slow and arranging everything as best I can with the fog in my mind from Tangier and smoke and all and Bruce gone too. Thank Eulalee for fronting the money to you. Write me a note at Ratato's N.Y. place which is where I'll be if I clear customs—burn this letter, of course. Love, Peggy

My dear Inny

Who would believe it but here I am in N.Y. encore and Allen called the other night but they told him I was in Tangier thank god which is where I was so it makes sense I'm sure but it is really a rush to say the least.

Why did you dream you were shooting H with me? Did Ratato ever tell you about our shooting H in his apartment or actually Bruce not me? Anyway I know last time I wrote I didn't tell you about all the morphine I'd been shooting and am now coming down off because I didn't know if you would trust me with all that money etc. but here I am.

Not to mention that Bruce took too much H on top of a weak speedfreak heart and died right next to me in bed and I was on H that night too and the police came and I had to get the works out of the house and answer the questions and not give anyone away. I can't stop thinking about it which is why I am out of Morocco and not just pouring all that money you sent into my veins but one look at the city makes me want to go back tomorrow. Anyway when I get West maybe it will be different and you will be a good influence on me.

This is Monday morning and yesterday I departed Tangier via avio with 9 (nine!) kilos of Ahmed's best hashish and walked through customs without a hitch—this is too much—I looked very straight—eight kilos are coming as we have arranged to San Diego and the ninth—or at least half of it—will come to you with me and we can play hide and seek to see what part of Peggy's body it's

(131)

secreted on hmmm. Please throw away this letter.

I'll probably try to call you later tonight but in case I can't get you or something I write. My parents rather intelligently took one look and asked if I'd go see a shrink. The sun is rising over central park—too much! I'd like to see it rise over the casbah but actually it only sets there and rises over the medina. Inez my love we must get out of this country before it is too late and I'm really serious— sooo much happens and we don't know anything about it which is really too much I mean it is not the same thank god in heaven-Hamdu-Allah.

But NY is also too much and I can't wait to score some good clothes and maybe cocaine although I foolishly left my syringe at Tangier with friends to use and I am sort of on cold turkey but doubt I will remain so because I like being dead too much. We all have different poisons as they say.

Dad was going to send the American Consul after me and then I surprised him by calling him from my mother's house where we'd been doing the old suitcase switch trick. I enclose the tickets so you can pick it up. And here I am. What a rush. What a strange trip—

Love, Peggy

Rainbo Woman has the wheel in hand. Hands. Out of L.A. past Disneyland's snowcapped peaks. Then down Highway Five, which snakes around the Cascade Mountains from Seattle through the Yosemite range and into California's central valley, next through that great belly of freeways known as metropolitan Los Angeles, coming out somewhere near the San Diego zoo, then dropping on down to Mexico for the dope runs of west coast college kids in their VWs. Geography made easy.

Inez Riverfingers in her Rainbo Woman cloak, driven mad by sex like every other flower child or young Republican. Driven mad not only by sex but by the endless nights spent writing a pornographic novel on her platform in the abandoned sunday school. Maybe reckless, but no fool.

(135)

The car is a rented Mustang, she is careful not to speed, she hopes her Rainbo disguise will save her, at least going down, from the vigilance of the Committee. It is rush hour and raining. She is alone, with the radio out of Pasadena doing its best to keep her sweat level down.

Do you wait out there, my friends, with your feathers already stuck in your hatbands? Where are your silver bullets, your fast Fords, your blue bellybuttoned lawmen?

It could be that the Committee, although it knows something is up, is fooled (by the friends who are having a party tonight at the sunday school, the careful subterfuge) and are unaware that she has left and turned on the ignition of this little American job Naomi Riverfingers rented for the week and won't bring back for another three days, parked in a side street about a mile from Burbank proper. After all, Peggy walked through Customs with the eight kilos in the bottom of a suitcase not unlike the one Inez is about to pick up at the San Diego Greyhound station.

Labyrinth of careful tracking and side tracking! We are the *ubermench* and can do anything if we have been careful to note that they are as good at backtracking and have studied as much behavioral psychology as we, if not more. We are the *uberwomen*. We can outfight them. We can outwit them. These may not seem like the battles of a true revolution. Certainly smuggling hash for personal gain has nothing to do with class struggle.

An unknown man (Ratato) sends a suitcase by Greyhound to San Diego; he arouses no suspicion. He sends the receipt 1002-69 to Inez Riverfingers in an envelope addressed to "San Fernando Blondie" at the Gay Liberation Office in West L.A., the one where Inez has never gone. The envelope is brought over to the main office two days after its arrival, where Inez puts it in her pocket.

Meanwhile, Peggy Warren, whose very existence the Committee doubts, sends a small black parcel, uninsured, via TWA. All airlines and bus stations have of course a check list on names: "If a woman named Peggy Warren sends a package to Los Angeles let the package go through but let us know immediately and stall her as long as possible so that we can follow her and obtain photographs for our records." Cops and robbers, the romance of the dollar and the barons of wallstreet—how to make a fast buck and elude them still and never have to lie low while making love and drinking champagne.

It is not Peggy who sends the package but her little sister Denise, which is what the Committee finds out upon tailing the young woman from the TWA airfreight office. They realize then that Peggy Warren, if she exists (and maybe she does after all, they are thinking), has slipped from their fingertips and is possibly not in New York but en route to western America via thumb and alias, impossible to track down. But they will get Inez the minute she picks up that parcel.

So they have an agent waiting at TWA for *anyone* who claims it, and they have a casual watch over Inez's house set up, one that will not arouse suspicion, but will just look like the local cops harassing the local freaks, a typical California diversion.

(137)

The friends are making dinner in the old sunday school and yell into Inez every once in awhile, who is writing in her room. What the Committee cannot of course know is that it is not Inez at all, but a friend who is there typing.

Inez is in the Mustang driving to San Diego. She is wearing a simple black skirt and flowered blouse, a blond wig and lipstick. The secret life of the transvestite, she thinks, forty miles outside of San Diego at sixty mph. A woman whose self-image has nothing to do with sex-appeal toothpaste (or everything to do with sex-appeal toothpaste), a woman, that is, in revolt against the feminine, simply dons the workday disguise of America's secretaries and is safe. She laughs.

The Committee couldn't possibly believe that I am fool enough to think that if they can't catch Peggy they can't catch me. They must realize it's too simple, that the suitcase at TWA couldn't possibly contain the hash. That I would never go there knowing how much they know, and let them stop me as soon as I get on the San Diego Freeway and do a search.

On the other hand, they have no idea that I am on this road to San Diego, in a Mustang in Naomi's name; that a suitcase looking innocent enough and which could easily be traced to a non-existent man on West 78th Street would contain eight kilos of hash, and that a woman with identification bearing the same last name of the man who insured the package (for the sake of the game the man said he was William Burroughs) would pick up that suit-case, drive a hundred fifty miles into L.A., leave the car parked in a school lot in Burbank, the suitcase still in the trunk; where she would be joined by a friend, change the skirt for a pair of jeans while keeping the wig on, drive to the not quite so abandoned sunday school where by then fifteen people are dancing and drinking beer, walk into Inez Riverfinger's room, switch clothes and wig with the girl so earnestly typing, and go out to join the party.

There are fifteen people there at my place, where are your informers? Where is your art, your craft? All those years of college and Peggy's Ellery Queen novels have paid off, you idiots. *You idiots!* Can you hear me? I hope not.

An old black guy hands the suitcase to Inez in the Greyhound station. It is 6:45 p.m. and the place is mobbed with people taking buses to Mexico, to

L.A., Las Vegas, S.F., to Arizona for the sunrise over the Grand Canyon, anywhere, darling, only let us just get away. O anything, Lord, even celibacy, just let me get away!

It is hard not to speed down Highway Five in the rare evening rain. She pulls at the nail of her ringfinger on her left hand until it is bleeding, although up until the ride back she has been wearing simple white gloves, like Mickey Mouse in the cartoon strips.

"I always thought," she later told Peggy as they bought each other drinks in San Francisco, "that the one thing I would always make sure of if I ever committed a crime, was that I would wear gloves and leave no fingerprints anywhere. I learned from the movies that they've undone wiser women than us, old buddy."

Peggy Warren leaned over the table and kissed her. Inez continued, sipping her Bloody Mary, "I even made sure to wipe them off the steering wheel." *(139)*

Peggy Warren: 5'2", 98 lbs, naturally blond hair, well-proportioned, creases around the corners of her mouth, habitual tea drinker, occasional affected English accent, speedreads detective novels and French literature, does bit nude roles and photo spreads (under the counter), was twenty when she got to San Francisco that June.

She had nearly a pound and a half of hashish, going for at least seventy-five dollars an ounce, contained in a special belt that hooked onto her underwear and slipped neatly between her legs. It had the one drawback of somewhat limiting her sexual activities while on the road, getting rides from the University ride boards (the last one had been a good one—straight from U. of Michigan to San Jose), hitching, and short bus rides.

She immediately calls up Eulalee Riverfingers, Inez's roommate from her first year at Reed—a stable, independently wealthy (enough so as to front Inez two thousand dollars even though she disapproved of the whole adventure), dancer taking classes at the University of California. No one in Eulalee's entire life ever even considered stopping her car or watching her apartment. There was an extra room then at Eulalee's and Peggy was welcome to stay there, Eulalee said over the phone, for as long as she liked. Later on Eulalee was filled in on some of the details.

Naomi Riverfingers, black hair and violet eyes (you remember), takes the suitcase to her father's house in Beverly Hills, and returns the Mustang to Hertz after two days. Dear Hertz, number one in our hearts, always, for this.

It is not at all unusual for three or four friends to drop by her house in an evening, and they do, quietly, getting together some instruments to play a little classical music. Naomi likes classical music (Bach) and concrete poetry. When she grows up, she says, she's going to be the dancer who puts red moons back into sewers, so that drunks will have the proper kind of mirrors.

Proliferation of names, of characters! Where does this one originate, what's the relation, how is it they all move in and out of each other's lives, thrown against each other in spiritual locker rooms, supplying uncertifiable amounts of indefinite qualities everyone longs for as they press their heads to the movie screen, hungering for their daily supplement of silver or sulphur?

I cannot tell you. One day Inez meets Naomi, Naomi Inez. Inez meets Abby, Peggy, Holly, Celeste, Natasha, Delphine, Eulalee, Mazie, they meet each other and others still. No one can articulate what, in secret, they take when they go.

When you look down into the river, suddenly it changes. Women cloaked in snow, women wrapped with black moss, surface, stretching, water shucked off their strong shoulders. Women walk out of the river and stare at each other. Some reach. Some shudder and turn into the woods or back to the river.

Naomi sells hash for Inez six months after they met. That is hardly the point. There are captions (young girl goes wrong) but it is only through their defiance that the captions matter. Together they walk through the suburbs. Alone, through the row houses, screaming at dogs. Families are gathered around t.v.'s. But these women will not own houses, are strangers to that kind of family. Their fingers struggle toward each other, webbed with sticky water. Some fingers meet, some don't. Three years later they will see each other (Naomi and Inez) at a film festival in New York, exchange addresses, never write. Born in the same cold stream, they disappear.

But this story has a happy ending, more or less. Rainbo Woman has pulled a caper. Everybody will make money and live happily ever after and the rotten, male-supremacist system will be smashed in the teeth again.

Everything is running smoothly. The Committee, although it has watched Inez's friends for the past two months, never had any particular reason to single out Naomi, and never did. The hash goes pretty much piecemeal—pounds for $900, half pounds for $475, ounces for between $60 and $100, grams for $5 or $10—or for nothing, if they were good enough friends. After eleven days of this quiet procedure Naomi has close to $19,000 in her dresser drawer, and a couple of ounces of hash left over.

"Keep that," Inez said, counting the money. "How much do I owe you?"

"You don't owe me anything, Inez. It was fun. This hash is still worth at least $300 if I don't smoke it all first."

"How about $500?"

"Jesus, what'll I do with $500?"

"Come away with me. Buy a new truck and we'll put together a traveling circus. We'll have a gypsy caravan. We'll write plays, Naomi, we'll make love as the sun comes up."

"Inez . . ."

"Okay. Here's the money. Have a good time and don't get *too* stoned."

Goodbye, Naomi. Maybe in a couple of years you will understand what I mean. All this money in my hand is making me very tough. I've never seen so much money and right now it is brighter in my mind than the thought of your hair sweeping my body.

Besides, Peggy is waiting for me in San Francisco. We have games to play, weeks of going to the movies and having front row seats for the Cockettes, getting drunk and finger fucking. But Peggy is not whom I ever really loved, though she is my cohort and companion; I would like it to be you, Naomi, coming. To wake in the mornings and push our heads through truck curtains at the sunrise in Death Valley, with its dry, cool desert morning, and run my cheekbones down your rib cage, make poems from the curls of your hair on my pillow, my arms, my breasts. I would like to forget about Abby, or remember Abby totally in you, be seventeen again.

I close my eyes and fear. I stand in Naomi's bedroom and I have so many ideas about why I love her that I have no idea. She has beautiful breasts that swing on her thin torso, her hair is black and goes down straight to the cleft of her rear. In *(143)* November, Naomi, it rained and I dreamed that you came into my room breathless, with a leaf sticking to your forehead, and we loved each other there suddenly, with no explanations for it. More images. More uncertainty.

In her father's house, with her piano and her paints (the captive princess), I have no way of knowing, following a train of thought that floats with birds' eggs and the extraordinary names of beetles in and out of the consciousness of her own small life, which has carved in the wood of my fantasy woodshed "Naomi was here" (among the others). She won't read that sentence there, won't know the texture of that wood, the needs that brought it there, to the imagination, to the dream of life which wakes us in the middle of the night thinking no no no more of this, I will never make love again if I spend my whole life lying on this platform, *thinking* about making love, *thinking* about telling her, never saying anything, offering tea to the forehead-leafed child who opens my door.

(Three years later, walking out of the New Consciousness Film Festival at the Whitney Museum, a woman in the front row calls to Inez. Inez stares at her. "I'm Naomi, remember?" They exchange addresses, but they don't write.)

"Take care, Naomi. If anyone ever asks you about Inez Riverfingers, she never existed. She was a Walt Disney cartoon character, an image from a poem some friend of yours wrote."

"You know, Inez, you have a talent for being pretentious." Naomi's eyes, which are violet, look at Inez for a long time. They smile. There is a long silence.

So Inez says, the little speech she has been preparing, "I guess this is how I think about our friendship, Naomi. At first it was chance, then circumstances, then necessity that held us together in this—proximity. Now all the deals are over. It has to be free will, a choice, to keep being friends with each other."

"That's a good way to put it, Inez. I want to be your friend. I'll write you care of Eulalee." Check. Nothing to do but go out the door.

"Okay, buddy, any time you need me, you can probably find out where I am through her—or just use your intuition. I'm here in the world for you, you know what I mean?"

"I know, Inez. I just need some time to understand what I'm doing. I can't take anybody's word
for anything, because everybody still thinks I'm a
kid, and I don't trust them to tell me what they
mean. I trust you sometimes, Inez, but I have to
find out for myself. Really. You understand that,
don't you? Didn't you have to, too?"

"Yeah. It's true. I had to. I'll miss you though.
Promise to write me."

"Sure. Drive carefully."

"Ok. Take care—and thanks again. I trust the
secrets of this affair are safe—you vill not crack
under torture?"

They hugged each other in the nearly smogged
out moonlight. Inez got into her truck and drove
home, stopping at the all-night grocery store to buy
some beer.

(145)

Inez Riverfingers Writes a Letter
to Abby in Israel

Abby, this is the fifth bottle of beer and you
know drinking makes me write. I have $18,468 in
my pocket. I have never seen so much money in my
life. No one (not even the Committee) will ever
believe any of this is true. I will be labeled a
perverse antisocial beast and will be sent to
Behavior Control for retraining.

I am leaving Los Angeles tomorrow for Berkeley,
so they won't have a chance to figure out a way of
trapping me here.

They may be right anyway. I may be crazy. But I don't want to think about it now; all I want is to relax for a while and forget about art and academics and politics and hope. I want to play gender games with Peggy and I want to drink as much beer as I can hold and be able to take taxis home and I want to go to the movies and the bars and make believe the big city of San Francisco is my sandbox. Isn't that the great American dream? Isn't that my right?

I, Inez Riverfingers, bearded lady, mother of god, sit on this platform for the last time, and realize that I have forgotten how to play. I have forgotten. I take myself so seriously now. You hear me sigh? Just like old times. Dammit, Abby, it's been over a year since I left you in N.Y. Tonight opening my door I half expected to see you there, waiting for me, on the bed.

Fact, that's all. Fact for the sake of fiction and fiction for the sake of fact, but no pleasure and no messing around. The other night, for instance, I went to bake bread with some friends: I organized it smoothly and efficiently, ladled out the ingredients, etc. But when they were kneading the dough they started to make sculptures of voluptuous women with raisin nipples, they molded cunts with delicate gentleness, they gave the bread women tiny bread children, then flattened them out again. They created hermaphrodites and made bad sexual buns. They sculpted the heads of Balzac. I was bored. Couldn't get into it. They thought I was angry with them, when I left, giving instructions for what to do when they finished playing. Angry! Only at myself, that I couldn't join, that I wanted nothing except the simple, factual thing itself: the loaves of bread made.

I have $18,468 in my pocket. It seems now like a very small sum of money for the risks we took. The president of General Motors earns that much money in a week. General Motors vs. General Mothers, place your bets, friends, it's this week's special televised bargain confrontation. The winner wins.

I have been careful enough to leave no evidence except the memoirs of a lunatic (yours truly). Just like there is no fact that can prove to me that I lived with you for two years, that you lived with me, that we lived as lovers, that there was something enjoyable about it, for both of us, at least in the beginning. Not a trace.

Everyone I suppose must go through true love once, but once should be enough to know that as illusions go, true love's one of the worst. And keeps us from our friends, our work . . .   (147)

The missions of ancient California flicker their clay in the hot sun. East to Death Valley National Monument and the Dirty Sock Mineral Pool, West to Big Sur and Castroville, artichoke capital of the world.

Gas needle on 3/4, oil pressure doing fine, tires new, brakes relined, Inez Riverfingers the first leans elbow-ward into the wind from the high seat of her panel truck named Harriet, which is white and green, and grins.

Grins all the way from L.A. to Berkeley, picking up people on the road. "Where are you going?"

"Berkeley."

"Hop in, you're in luck this time."

And the kids from the university, everyone has mutual friends, they buy crates of fresh strawberries, they tell stories about their experiences on the road, it is a very shiny Friday in the world.

The hills and lakes bulge with purple and yellow flowers, the very winding road through Big Sur shouts them out of their panel truck to climb, strangers, together, to watch the sea, to record in the back of their eyes this sun going down, to hope to see whales fume out at sea (they don't), to gather giant cattails which they stick in the frame of the truck so that driving down the road the heads of them break open, throwing out trails of seed across the banks, picking wildflowers to hang on the rear-view mirror. Wonderful tidal August! Inez watches her hitchhikers play against the waves and rock.

Eighteen thousand three hundred dollars are rolled tightly up in a cardboard tampax tube, and lie quietly in her vaginal tract. Put it in and forget about it—you too can be really safe. And she is, she is.

What a homecoming! What hugging! What a smell of honeysuckle in the air! Blake Street in Berkeley, with the dogs chasing the car and the time around ten p.m. and all the hitchhikers safely deposited . . .

But carefully, carefully. Just because there is no

trouble doesn't mean the dogs of the Committee can't smell money even when it's hidden in a cunt. Inez parks her truck on the other side of Berkeley, down around 10th Street, near another friend's place, above a sign which says: Chinese Hand Laundry (the Chinese have long since abandoned this part of Berkeley, it's the blacks, the poor whites and the hippies here for at least ten years now).

Riverfinger on Riverfinger, streaming from the night hallways, watcha brought me mommy? Another Riverfinger home to dinner, hiya Mazie, Hi Bill, howdy everyone, let's have a drink. (Eulalee and Peggy are still on Blake Street, waiting for the phone to ring. Inez is not that punctual.)

What a homecoming! What hugging! What could Inez be thinking? Why hasn't she gone to them? Too soon, that's what. Everything's too easy. I like my world more covered with jagged pieces of broken danger. I want chases, narrow escapes, a (149) pain that borders on suicide every minute, I want us to be desperate, how else will I justify anything, how can you enjoy a half gallon of Gallo chianti if it's not spiced with despair? How can you feel *angst* if all goes well and there is back-slapping and laughter? *Where are your policemen your tear gas your riots, Berkeley? Where are your snares, your tortures, your fabled instruments of mutilation, love?*

Inez kisses Bill and hugs Mazie, they talk about old times, new times. She does not tell them about the hash but promises to take them out to dinner sometime.

"How about now?" asks Bill. It must be lean days above the Chinese Hand Laundry.

Down at Spengler's, the best seafood place in walking distance, Inez orders another bottle of wine.

"Can I see your i.d.?" Inez smiles and pulls out her California driver's license, upon which her photograph smirks like the whore in Fellini's *8½*. Smirk, go ahead, you have the right, who has run and sold eight kilos of hash and at whom the waiter has squinted, thinking "that kid—." That kid! Whom Bukowski shouted at, "Betcha want to lay me right now!" Who has escaped the knives of Baltimore rapists (come on baby give me some pussy), that kid who hangs out in gay bars and listens to soft young girls talk about the circus and their art and how they want always to live for the moment, as they sew up trouser legs and Inez watches them with her slightly lecherous and embittered eye. Smirk, go ahead, do a sexy little lip rub with your pink tongue and then stick it back between your molars, you deserve it, kid.

"Okay, I guess you're okay." You better believe it you paternal runt—you look to me like you've spent your whole life snuggling up to the head-waiter but never getting off. But after all, I could be wrong—we all seem to have our secret lives, don't we?

Mazie orders lobster newburg. Bill orders rainbow trout. Inez has broiled lobster. This must be what it's all about.

"Are you sure you can afford this?"

"I can afford anything now. I'm rich." They're curious. They watch her carefully. No more stealing pennies from the Reed College Coffee Shop, now it's the big time—what happened? Inez laughs and halfway through her lobster orders another bottle of wine. Bottle bottle down the throttle strip the gears of the cosmos I am breaking life apart with my shoulders with my terrible teeth. I want to get back to Blake Street with the hugging and the homecoming and Eulalee and Peggy and the dogs barking and the bed where at least me and Peggy and maybe Eulalee too boy that would be good Eulalee with her beautiful brown round breasts and her trained dancer's strength might join us once in the round, in the flesh.

"Well, have a good dinner?" Inez, having consumed a good gallon of wine by this time is having trouble controlling her muscles. Bill and Mazie furrow their foreheads a great deal. What has happened to Inez? And what is this mysterious source of money? Ah, who would suspect that the gentle tampax, so well designed for feminine protection, the sturdy cardboard housing we know so well, could actually turn into a spigot that would buy blood red wine for the rest of your life? For another year, at least.

"All right if I use your phone?" From the porch on 10th Street, Berkeley glistens like Cibola in the night.

"Eulalee? It's Inez. I am very very very very drunk. What I want you to do is drive out down Ashby, get on the freeway, get off at University and come back up a couple blocks past 10th Street and I'll be there hitching and it will uh it will—look you know like you're just picking up a hitchhiker. Because because that's what I said. Don't shit around with me, Eulalee, I'm a desperado. Watch out I don't fall beneath your wheels, though, I am, in case I have not mentioned it, very very drunk. *Hasta luego*." Inez hangs up the phone.

"Is it okay if I leave my truck behind your house for a couple weeks?"

"Sure, but why, Inez?"

"Well, you know, I don't want the Committee to know I am staying with Eulalee. And I don't want them to know that Peggy Warren is here."

"Why?"

"On account of because it's a dangerous business and hell fire and the shadows of minnows. Is a big dark secret, okay?"

"Okay, what is it, Inez?"

"It's the darkest of all the secrets a Riverfinger has to keep. If you give it away you will be drummed out of the Riverfingers forever and ever so help me god."

"Inez, quit farting around and tell us what's going on!"

"Okay, okay. This is the thing: me and Peggy did this dope deal—Tangier. It's too long a story for right now, some other time when I'm sober. But it's all very risky and now we have a little money and are going to have us a good time in the big city and then drive off down the road in search of America or Utah or Rainbow Trout or maybe Abigail Riverfingers my one and only true love and then we will retire to the woods and catch wall-eyed pike which is the only fit life for a bona fide fried dyke. Got that?"

Mazie and Bill are laughing. Mazie makes one of those typical gestures of straight women who think it will show how far they've come, it will be an act of solidarity, they will reach an arm to their gay sisters, reach to kiss their lesbian friends to show, to prove it, they have no prejudices, they aren't up-tight at all.

How shall I convince her, how can I begin to tell her she should be ready, if she is going to stand there kissing, to be asked what she means, to be aware or else not kiss at all? Mazie, in one of those gestures, kisses Inez quite typically and laughs more.

"Okay, okay," Bill says. He is very impressed, because he has never had more than a hundred dollars in his hands his whole life. He is a poor boy who picks his guitar and drives an ice-cream truck and used to hang around Reed College, so meeting Mazie, a freshman from Maryland (dropped out) and they came to live together above the Chinese Hand Laundry. Now Mazie studies karate, is an apprentice carpenter, and has become an expert shoplifter so that everyone eats well enough, with the added help of the United States Government food stamp plan. They are relatively poor folk, and support half a dozen drifters, who sway back and forth across the country, in and out of Berkeley.

"Can we use your truck while it's here?"

"Why, William, I am ash-shamed I did not make it clear to you that Robbing Hood is alive again in the world and having a good time. Here's the car key, here's—let me see—" (not wanting to have to go to the bathroom and open the tampax spigot from between her thick thighs Inez decides to give them most of what is left from the trip expenses) "Okay, here's like eighty-five dollars for gas and stuff."

"Inez, we can't take that."

(153)

"Shut up, you jerks, of course you can. It's evilly-got money and I got plenty. Go to the movies or something. Just be careful when you drive my truck because I love it as much as any woman I ever loved, pistons, rings and transmission. But if, uh, you have an accident, or anything, Eulalee's phone number's in the phone book. But try not to call, I'll get in touch with you. Got that?"

"We've got it. Boy. Fuck. Thanks a lot, Inez."

"Any time, any time. Now I have to go fall down the stairs and into the street so that Eulalee can run over me. Listen, if the Committee comes and asks you any questions, tell them I just left the truck here and went to stay with some friends in San Fran and you don't know who and I didn't act unusual."

"And we don't know anything. Sure thing, Inny. Don't worry about it. A Riverfinger in need is a Riverfinger, indeed."

Inez trips on the stairway, Mazie rushes down to help her, and Inez leans against her shoulder until they get to the doorway.

"Thanks," Mazie says.

Inez looks at her for a second. Decides against making anything of it. "No. Thank *you*," she says.

"Goodnight, be careful."

 "Wanta ride, kid?"

"Why certainly, lady, that is just why I got my thumb out so that you in your dad's rich car could just come and suck on it for awhile, sweet Eulalee of my harbor's beam—"

"Jesus, Inez are you plastered."

Slam door. Roll head down and stick window out it. No. Roll down window and stick out head. Right the second try. Wind against stretched nerves cools them down to a slow burn. The anesthetist's assistant, Eulalee.

"Eulalee, do you remember when I came to see you in Berkeley just fourteen months ago, down from visiting Reed College. All the night before on that seventeen-hour ride I began to think about a certain way you have of hugging everyone, how maybe you would hug me that way and you did and we went to someone's apartment in Oakland where I drank a whole gallon of red wine and said: I have something to tell you. I have drunk-drank-drinken a whole bottle of wine to say will you sleep with me? It was the hardest thing in the world to say that. That was before I had read that there were other—women like me in the world and Abby had left me and there I was on a splintery bench drunker than I am now with my face out the window in the soused wind, winding around the curves of night city of Shattuck with its yellow lights damn these yellow lights, it looks like a stage set for a horror movie, Eulalee. And then, three months later you said to me, 'You know, just as I began to think that maybe I would like that—' "

"Like what?" Eulalee asks, smiling and concentrating on the street.

"Sleeping with you. Just when you thought you wouldn't mind sleeping with. You just wanted to hear me say it."

"Okay, go on."

"Just then and we were on the bed together and

you were rubbing my back with your hand—I was rubbing your back with my hand jesus I am losing the thread of this. Just as you were about to take me up on it, I started to puke over everything." Eulalee laughed then, looking sideways from the road at her friend. "Well, I was scared shitless that you'd take offense, if I asked you. Mostly straight women do," Inez said.

"I was just offended that you should puke over everything and I ended up cleaning it up."

Good Eulalee, sweet Eulalee, what a homecoming, what hugging.

"Hey, Inez, you are being very quiet all of a sudden, I hope you're not going to be sick."

"If I be sick, I just vomit out the edge of the car and it be no trouble to sponge it off daddy's Buick in the morning. I'll do it."

"Inez." Eulalee put her arm around Inez's shoulders briefly. "I'm really glad to see you, Inny, even if you are drunk. I miss you when you're away."

"But you won't make love to me when I'm here."

"Inez . . ."

"I'm sorry, Eulalee. I'm just drunk, right? I love you very much, you being always a good friend to me and I always coming to you weeping or bleeding and you always pulling off all your clothes and holding me to your breast until I fall asleep beside you. But I am happy now, how will I get you to touch me if I am not in *need* of hugging?"

"You will ask me, like you just did," Eulalee laughed again and took her arm back off the steering wheel, this time holding Inez's hand. "You have the right to ask, little friend, I have the right to say no when that's what my boundaries are, is it a deal?"

"It's a deal, lady." Inez was happy then, just like she had been happy years before, when she was a junior at Highland and had never even seen Abby. She and some friends went into New York for Christmas and got very drunk at the Waldorf and she fell all over the sidewalk and these beautiful women, her friends, held her hands and it seemed to her the highest point of her sexual life. That two tall beautiful wasp women, her friends, would hold the hands of a fat Jewish kid by the name of Inez Bramanoi who was disgustingly drunk as only sixteen-year-olds can be. They held her hands all through the subway ride to Jamaica and she loved them and their love for her made her love herself all at once and she wanted to be drunk forever.

Eulalee held Inez's hand all the way up University and Shattuck and Blake until she had to park the car. Inez kissed it, once, pretending to be a knight of the round table.

(157)

"My lady of the warm bed, of the palace of wisdom, I thank you eternally for having the extreme patience and goodness to be my friend."

Eulalee smiled. Who knows what she was thinking? I always hoped, Eulalee, can you hear me? I have always hoped that although I came to you wounded and leaned on all your resources, your strength, time and time again, and although I hated you sometimes for sleeping beside me as if we had been married forty years and never daring to use your mouth or fingers against my body and making me afraid to use mine on yours, for the times I would sleep in the same room with you while you fucked your boyfriend of the moment and I pretended it was cool with me, I thank you anyway, Eulalee, because you are a good friend to me, always at the gates of my entrances and exits into the world.

But god knows what you are thinking about me and my adventures tonight as you pilot me through Berkeley to Peggy Warren who will sleep with me in your spare room, after you kiss and hug us both goodnight. You will decide that you had better not rush into anything impulsively that you might not be ready for, and I can understand that, fogged as I am at this minute.

"Eulalee, I love you," says Inez as Eulalee shuts off the ignition of her car.

"I love you too, Inez." They hug each other on the front seat and because Inez is drunk she makes as if to french kiss Eulalee, who shakes her head a little as she would to a child into the cooky jar again, and then accepts tongue between her rows of perfect teeth, probing the sister tongue. Inez is touched by this. Touched, although Robert Peterson who was the instructor of creative writing at Reed College hated the word when it appeared in one of her late adolescent poems: touched. The kiss is a short one and Inez puts her head on Eulalee's shoulder.

I have always loved things that were gone: Janis Joplin because she o.d.'d, Edith Piaf because she died on my birthday, the trains because no one rides them anymore, but I love you because you are here, the great shingle on my Western roof—Inez wrote on Eulalee's bathroom mirror in chapstick.

"Inez!" Peggy's blond voice and thin arms encircle wide Inez who stumbles to her. Peggy! What a reunion! What a homecoming! What risks! What success! What hugging! What dogs barking! What honeysuckle! How drunk! How happy! Let's just go to bed!

"Do you have your period, Inny?"

"Oh, fuck, that's the money. Pull it out. I feel like I am a pinata."

Peggy Warren with her fingers like the beaks of birds sucking juice from ripe fruit, reached in between the pink lips of Inez's vagina, pulled the cardboard tube down slowly while softly twisting the nipple on her right breast, just rubbing it, really, naked as both were, in bed.

ooooo Peggy money sometimes Peggy you know people these days Peggy I think they underestimate the pleasure oooo the pleasure that money can bring ahhh

Peggy has it out now, the white cardboard roll, softening now, covered in yellow-white excretions, from its ride inside Inez. Peggy opens it up, now it holds no folds of white absorbent cotton, designed specifically for the woman who has a larger flow, but a great moist wad of green paper.

"Shall I cover your nakedness with the results of our evil ways and days, Ahmed's best hash turned into green American dollars, shall I rub every sweet billow and crevice of your body until you smell of the smell of men's sweat at Fort Worth and your own come? Huh, Inez?"

Inez is in the process of passing out from the wine and the ride and the release of being in bed again with a good friend. No more empty platform nights. She only gurgles a little assent.

But Peggy is very awake. She has all the money in her hand and nearly a pound of hashish left. She spreads the money out, more for her own satisfaction than Inez's, as Inez is already beyond pleasure, putting out to the black oceans of unconscious.

Five hundred dollar bills over the nipples, mouth, crotch, armpits. Patterns of hundreds and fifties, over the arms, the thighs, the belly button. Peggy, earlier in her career as a human being, had been a photographer and managed to retain that detached eye in times like these, the photographer's layer of separation from experience, so that the experience can be rearranged and recorded permanently in its most interesting and esthetic state. She made mandala patterns with twenty dollar bills (the smallest) and because there were so many left she had Inez be the human center spoke of a mandala that stretched its money wheel across the double mattress.

Bodies and money, sex and drugs, money and

Editor's Note: The reader will note that fitting this much money in a tampax tube is an impossible feat. However, Inez refuses to divulge her methods while the Committee is still at large.

bodies (again). We have more knowledge from the mystic East than knowledge of drugs and houkas; the mandala, the naked body at the center of the mandala, prove it. We have made such scars on each other in our confusions, we have suffered for images of being women and hip children. Now we can think about our wounds, how to mend them. Peggy Warren thinks, in the moment of silence, in the moment of clear meditation, looking at Inez's decorated body.

She was suddenly sick of men. For a long time she had studied enjoyment. But the lack of feeling in all those past lovers had built up a great anger. She was glad to be here with Inez, who was expansive and childish with all this money, romantic enough to stick it up her crotch.

Inez would protect her without being motherly. Inez would let her do what she wanted. One night Peggy could put on jeans and workshirt while Inez would put on the maxi-hippy dress with the low front Celeste had made years before, the only dress Inez still owned. Peggy would play a tough, skinny little butch taking mother earth out for a drink.

The next night, Inez could wear the jeans, open the car doors, be mean and suave, say "my dear" a lot, and Peggy would wear a blouse with a wide, soft pointed collar and a simple skirt. They would dance together, although Inez was bound to be a little awkward on the dance floor. Inez had only learned to dance after she started going to gay bars.

Peggy smiled. It was getting late—tomorrow they could think of ways to spend all that money, they could talk and make love and smoke hash and borrow Eulalee's car and go into the city. Inez could play indulgent dyke at the better shops; maybe Peggy could talk her into finding a way to score morphine or cocaine . . .

It doesn't matter, Peggy was saying to herself then, that Bruce was dead, that one face of one lover would begin to melt into the face of someone else somewhere and she was not sure anymore even what color their eyes had been, which she was always proud to remember long after their names.

Inez was soft, crazy, and understanding. She would not abuse Peggy, and she would somehow convince Abby to come back (Peggy had watched them one whole summer and was sure of it). Peggy had always wanted to live with Abby and Inez again, only this time it would be the three of them and she, Peggy, wouldn't lie outside the closed door, listening to them strain the bed springs. Between the three of them they could manage to work and protect each other and get along without men.

For Peggy there were definitely too many men in her memory. They were crowding in and shouting after her, pulling her skirt as she ran down the hard pavement of her hitchhike nightmares. She wanted to shut the lights and action out of all those scenes, she wanted to be taken care of gently, she wanted not to feel cheap and used and ugly, she wanted to be loved without the big forcefulness that even the gentlest men had put her through.

Here beside her the warm, passed-out body of Inez Riverfingers stirred a little as Peggy took all the bills off her body and the bed, and lay down beside her, resting her face in Inez's big breasts. Here it is safe, here is Inez, four years later, and Inez is generous and Inez says yes, yes Peggy, this embrace, I will say it is for you, these arms, these games we will play.

Peggy fell asleep and did not dream.

"Excuse us, please, but you are Miss Mazie Riverfingers, are you not?"

"Yes, I am. What do you want?"

"We are members of a Committee, and we are looking for one Inez Riverfingers, who, we believe, has left her car with you, although she is not staying here and we cannot ascertain her whereabouts."

"So?"

"We would like to ask you a couple questions if you don't mind."

"What if I do?" Out on the West Coast, women get tough quick. Or perhaps this is just a different generation than the one with the soft women and their bodices and angel food cakes.

"Well, we—uh don't mean to be personal or pry, but you see this Inez Riverfingers is of special concern to us because we have parts of a manuscript which leads us to believe that she is extremely disturbed, on the verge of a severe psychotic break, possibly suicidal. Her family is quite concerned, naturally, and have informed us that they will do anything within their power to help her out, which we see as a quite generous offer on their part, considering her extreme and persistent hostility toward them."

"You guys are full of shit."

(163)

"Please, Miss Riverfingers, don't make us do anything you would regret later. We're only trying to help her."

"What do you want to know?"

"Won't you let us in?"

"You've gotta be kidding. It's bad enough I'm letting you stand on my porch where the neighbors can see you."

"That attitude won't get you far, young lady. You too have parents that could be contacted and persuaded to believe things about your present—life situation that, properly phrased, might lead them to consider a similar course of action."

"Are you threatening me?"

"No. We just want you to be a little more realistic. Now, where *is* Inez Riverfingers?"

"I don't know."

"You're lying."

"Don't call me a liar, you cabbagehead! Inez is somewhere in San Francisco, I have no idea where. She left her car here because it's a hassle to have it in the city. I have no idea when she'll be back or if she'll be back. That's all I know and all you're going to find out unless you turn over every fucking barrel in a two hundred mile radius."

"Are we to infer that Inez left her truck here without any instructions?"

"You can infer what you damn please. If she calls I'll tell her to write her parents a letter. Now get lost."

"Miss Riverfingers, we would like you to understand that this is no light matter. The power of the Committee is much more far reaching than you seem to be willing to accept. We hope you realize that if you are ever under some special kind of scrutiny by any of our security branches, you will be treated with the utmost harshness. I say this only for your own good. There are ways you can alleviate the burden of your present difficulty—"

"I'm sick of listening to this garbage—get out. You make me sick!"

Mazie slammed the porch door on them, locked it from the inside, went around the front to lock the front door, and proceeded to put the bread in the oven and listen to James Taylor's new album.

"I wanta break that bitch's door down. That little cunt, who does she think she is?"

"You better not try it, Jimmy," said their spokesman. "She knows her rights and hasn't done anything yet we can really get her for. Aside from which, that little cunt, as you call her, is a brown belt in karate. God knows how we are going to find Inez, though, unless she comes to pick up her truck —and that guy drives it all the time—that means we have to station one person here, to keep a watch on the house, we have to get the lines tapped— that'll be easy—and we have to have men in cars that will follow either of those two characters. I guess we'll keep it up for a couple of weeks; if nothing turns up we'll have to drop it."

(165)

Telephone on 10th Street goes ring. Bill picks up the machine. "Oh, jesus, Inez, where are you? Where you been?"

"I'm in the city. We're in a department store and

I got bored so I thought I'd find out how things were going."

"Wait a second. I think the phone is tapped. The Committee was here."

"Fuck. What did they say?"

"Mazie talked to them. Here, she'll tell you."

"Hi, Inez? Listen, these guys come up to the door, all wearing suits, and they start asking me these questions about where you are and saying your parents were really freaked out about you and wanted to commit you. They started threatening me that they would get me committed if I didn't tell them and all that kind of shit."

"Bastards. What did you tell them?"

"Nothing. But the phone is tapped and they've been following us around and everything. What should we do?"

"I'm sorry to be putting you through all this hassle. I'm sick of those motherfuckers bugging my friends. You should keep the car, I'll write you a letter in a couple months."

"What?"

"If you don't want to keep it, sell it. I don't know. I'm leaving the city pretty soon but I have some things to take care of here. Probably I'll go to Canada. —Hey, fellas, if you're listening, why don't you stop grabbing? I haven't got your brass ring. Why, I'm only a small-fry queer in the great cogs of the coming American Revolution. I better hang up before they trace the call and come and get me. Assholes. Keep the car. I'll write you when I get where I'm going if I ever get there. If you sell it, keep half of the money and save me the other half. Okay?

"Okay. Listen, we'll try to sell it sometime this week so you can have the money when you leave. Okay?"

"Okay."

"Well, take care, Inny."

"Yeah, you too, Mazie. Thanks again, and thank Bill for me, will you?"

"Sure, goodbye."

Somewhere in the greasy bowels of the metropolitan telephone company, two agents of the Committee stare at each other.

"Dead end," the dark one says. "Personally, I don't understand why they're keeping this up, even if they think that Peggy Warren chick is with her, which I doubt. They don't even seem to have any money."

"Yeah, but they were in a department store and it could all be some kind of ruse, you know. Maybe they have enough money to just go out and buy another car in some fake name, which would certainly be easier than going through all this subterfuge. Otherwise, why wouldn't Inez just come out and give legal battle and be done with it?"

(167)

"I don't think she wants to face her parents; that's pretty obvious. You know these queers are all fucked up anyway. I guess she figures it's easier to play cops and robbers. But I really don't think there's any sense in keeping on her tail like this, Joe. She seems to have abandoned writing trash for the time being, anyway, and it doesn't seem like there was ever any narcotics shipment in the first place. She's scared or at least sick enough of being followed to be very quiet for awhile—she's already stopped working for the G.L.F., which is one way we can report that we've been effective, at least."

"Yeah, I guess. You sure about the narcotics?"

"Listen, it takes more organization to get that kind of thing underway. I think it was just one of those post-adolescent fantasies. This investigation is getting to be a waste of time and money."

"I think you're right. We'll keep an eye on that 10th Street apartment, though, just in case anything weird turns up, and tell her parents that we've failed to locate her, but have left messages with people who know her that she should get in touch with them as soon as possible."

"Right, that seems like the only thing to do."

Five days later, a young woman named Sylvia Stein appears at the 10th Street apartment, looks over the '61 International, buys it for four hundred dollars and departs. The Committee, after realizing that somehow Bill and Mazie have an address at which to send Inez the money, but that the money will be sent to her via a fake name and another of this endless progression of friends, and not having any information on Sylvia Stein that would link her to Inez, decides to forget about the whole thing for the time being.

Sylvia is Eulalee's young cousin. She signed the papers and left with the truck, Inez's joy, taking it to a body shop where she had it repainted brown.

"Why you want it to be brown, lady?" the mechanic asked.

"Well, I feel that brown is more—*my* color, you know. It's the karma of colors that keep your head together. And I don't like the idea of driving a truck that belonged to somebody else and was in the colors that were part of their karma, right?"

"Yeah, sure thing, lady." There sure are some weirdos in Berkeley these days.

When the paint job was done, Sylvia parked it behind her house, where it stayed until Peggy and Inez were ready to leave Eulalee's for their drive East, in search of Abby.

"You know what I was doing before we got into this escapade together, Peggy?"

"What, Inny?"

"I was writing a pornographic novel because I was bored. So I wrote forty pages, then I was bored with that too. Besides, it wasn't very pornographic."

Peggy kissed Inez on the cheek. Peggy was wearing a pair of tight, black bellbottoms and a man's turtleneck shirt. Inez was wearing her Indian print mother earth dress. They were walking down Haight Street arm in arm.

(169)

There is pleasure in being blatant. Here, world, I am a woman who loves other women. I love their games and their smells and their softnesses in bed. I love to walk arm and arm with them and tumble through all the disguises we can think of for one another, the end of gender identification.

I am happy on Haight Street, sitting in a small gay bar with a sign that reads: Pool For Ladies Only, Peggy Warren's little uneven teeth nipping my shoulder at a table in the corner. I am happy, what difference does any of this make to you, why are you even interested in it?

Who knows. We each have our reasons for wanting to know everything there is to know about women. She who has been mystery for centuries is coming out. We who have not made common cause since the fall of the great matriarchies, we are coming together (watch out).

It is Friday night. Women from all over the city and from the suburbs too come in to the few bars just for women and which only women inhabit, except for a few stray strangers who wander in by mistake and quickly leave again, a few habitual voyeurs, a few male gays who have friends here or who like to be among women with whom they feel safe.

Peggy used to go to guy's gay bars in New York all the time, because she found she could dance all night, which she loved to do, without having hands up her crotch or pinching her ass or fumbling with her boobs as it was when she danced with straight men. Once she even got on stage with the male stripper, and stripped along side of him, and all the boys were shocked to see that she really *was* a woman. Not having seen a woman undressed, some of them, except in bra and girdle ads in the *New York Times*, they were more interested in her anatomy than in their regular stripper (or the slides of nude men in various erotic poses, sometimes alone and sometimes with other men, that flashed on the wall continually in time to the music, creating a gay light show).

Inez had gone once with Peggy to one of those places, before Peggy had been in Tangier, but she hadn't liked it. "It made me feel like a voyeur, aside from which, I am not particularly interested in the male reproductive organs, though I have nothing against them, mind you."

Eulalee always shook her head when Inez went off to the city gay bars before, though now that she went with Peggy, Eulalee would just kiss them goodnight and go off to her boyfriends. Between Inez and Eulalee, before, there had always been a feeling that when Inez had to go gay bar hopping it was because somehow Eulalee had failed her. If only Eulalee could get it together to be Inez's lover, Eulalee often thought, then Inez would never have to search out a woman through those dark female jungles, strung with danger like candy canes on trees that have been sprayed with poison.

"Those who really suffer," Inez told Eulalee, "are the ones who stay home alone, who do not know where to go or who to talk to or that there even is anyone they can talk to, who think somehow a miracle will change them and make them straight, who fear the lord or their parents. Sometimes the women in the bars suffer, too, but not while they're in the bars. The bars are a sweet place, a place where we can dance and make out with each other, be open with our friends, make eyes at strangers, not worry about anything except how many drinks we can afford to buy, and which advances we want to accept. Even when we get tangled with women who are really into their roles, it's safe."

Eulalee, who was very wholesome, one might put it, who danced seriously for the sake of health and movement, whose biggest compulsion was ice cream, had a lot of trouble understanding what Inez told her.

It is Friday night. Women from all over the city and from the suburbs too come in to the few gay bars that are for women only, to be with each other, to dance and play pool, to get drunk and make scenes, to drop whatever pretense it is that they live with in order to survive and make money, and get down to the real business, the real intrigues, the real enjoyment of their lives.

Inez walked in, arm linked in Peggy's and began to smile a grin she only gave when in the bars. Everywhere is like love for her there, every table holds possibility, every encounter the mixture of decadence and innocence that make her happy. She would talk and look openly (it is already discovered, you are here) with every woman there.

One table might contain women who resembled (or were) the teachers she had been infatuated with as a child. At first the older women are intriguing, especially for that reason, that they should be similar to women one had admired and wanted as mother or lover (later on), and who had then engendered in one such shame, such penitence, such sorrow, feeling that these beautiful women, these emblems that studded one's most precious hours (the hours left alone for fantasy) would never, could never never, understand or reciprocate. Suddenly they have dropped the mask, the school teacher in her red dress asks you to dance with her and you surge with an enormous joy, tenderness and power.

But it is soon evident that my youth, if nothing

else about me, gives me too much power for the older ones. The games are too tedious—I am not looking for a mother, after all, someone who wants to baby me or who sees in me the lesbian they were in their youth and who want to regain that youth. Besides, it is unfair to say that it is more than a momentary impulse in them also, who are with their friends, and enjoy the steadiness of the lives they have come to.

I suppose that while my affection seems to me boundless, encompassing the whole world, while I dance in the arms of an older woman who might have been Miss Jacobs, the third grade drama teacher I never got over, or Sally, that friend of my mother's who would come to visit once a month and after she left I would stroke the sofa where she had sat, sniffing my palm as if her smell somehow really lingered there (deep childhood search for lost affection), while I dance and they hold my awk- *(173)* ward round body against them, it seems to me I could love them instantly and go off to their city flats, and share their life, and submit to their loving me, although I know it is not true.

Peggy dances on the other side of the room with a girl about her height who is strikingly beautiful. I smile at them and resolve to spend the rest of the evening as if I have never seen Peggy before, or had contracted amnesia at the door.

I move over to the bar section and buy a Bloody Mary. The bartenders are incredibly masculine and wear their hair in those slickbacked ducktail haircuts that people wore in the fifties. They wear work overalls or jeans, and stick their hands in their back pockets when they aren't busy, smoking Camels without ever taking them from their mouths unless someone orders a drink.

"That'll be a buck, kid," they say. They seem like icebergs, like caricatures and yet, at closing, their women or their friends come and talk to them and they are suddenly as sympathetic and kind, mopping up the bar, with no more money to haul in for the mafia, as the most gentle social worker in San Francisco. These women, I think, are my true foremothers. They became strong and independent in isolation. They may seem to me all caught up in roles, they may never agree with me about what's important, what a political act it is within the state to be a lesbian, an act of defiance—nevertheless, they committed that act and gave me the courage to commit mine. I love them.

A tall severe blond in a tailored severe gray suit sits down beside me.

"Let me dance with you." She has an accent that reminds me of Greta Garbo (oh, Greta Garbo, the only woman I ever *really* loved!). "Let me dance with you, I say," the woman in the suit says. I am a little drunk. I think maybe it is Greta Garbo in disguise, tripping me up with my own images. I agree.

Back out on the dance floor she presses me to her violently. Her hands push hard into my back, she runs her fingers up and down my neck, and rubs her head on that part of my breasts which is uncovered.

"I want it. I want it," she says. She is very drunk, more drunk than I, but I dig it that she should sound like Garbo, that she should thrust her chin at my chest and desire me with such spontaneous passion. "I want it, can you give it to me? Can you give it to me tonight? Tonight, tonight, darling, I want it. I love what you have. You understand what I am saying? I love it. You can give it to me if you want to, do you want to? Oh, I want it so much, please, I must have it." (*It* again, always *it*, the IT Girl and the *it* drink and how is *it* and what is *it* and can I have *it*, what is the secret of *it* and how many ways are there to say *IT*, IT IT, always IT.)

I am playing with this woman, I am considering going off with her, I am not sure, I am digging *it*. We go back to the bar and she buys me a drink. The bartenders take in everything under their strong, water-buffalo gaze. Over and over again she tells me how much she wants it, runs her hands along my arms and my breast. I start to reciprocate (having gone this far) and guide my palm along her thigh . . .

"Ow! Not there, that's my knife wound!" I am (175) considerably taken aback. A little frightened, even. No matter how much I respect tough women, I don't trust those who play with knives.

"Your knife wound?" I question, retreating.

"Oh yes, it's nothing, darling, I got into a little fight last night, that's all, you will come with me, won't you? I want it, I want it so badly, you must give it to me."

Her desperation over my body and her newly-uncovered tendency for duels seems to me a little dangerous. Perhaps more than a little. Not, at any rate, the kind of thing I want really to be involved in, I realize, sobering some. "Wellll . . ."

"Well, well what?" She responds immediately to

my change in attitude. Her eyes begin to penetrate me, seeking out any weakness she might use as a wedge against my reluctance.

"Well," I continue, coming out of my Peggy Warren amnesia. "I'm here with a friend, and I wouldn't want to leave her alone."

"You mean you have been playing with me all this time!"

"No, no it isn't that at all . . ."

"Darling, darling, I want it so badly—if you give it to me tonight maybe then we will go to Los Angeles if you want, or Mexico—" She strokes my hand as she says this and I burst out laughing. The idea of going to Los Angeles again seems like the funniest thing I have heard in years, coming as it does as part of a desperate and serious proposal by a woman who after all knows nothing about me.

"You think I am making jokes? No, really, I will do this—"

(176)

"No, you don't understand, I *am* with a friend, I don't want to leave her, she doesn't know how to drive the car."

"We could take her where she wants to go."

"No."

"What is it then? Someone has been telling you stories about me?" She is furious that I am turning her down and I am a little frightened. The bartenders don't move. "Have they told you I am a tough bastard? Well, I *am* a tough bastard. I am proud of that. *Why* don't you want me?"

"I guess I'm not into people being quite that tough," I say, trying not to hurt her, and realizing that perhaps I look tonight enough like a stereotyped femme that she really believes I am one—a soft, sloppy woman who wants a very masculine woman to take care of her, to be her boss. That makes me feel apologetic, because I am drunk and sad that I am not who she is looking for, I am sad she is looking in this particular way.

"I don't think I am really what you are looking for," I say. "Maybe my body, but I—I'm not really a femme, you know—I just like—dressing up sometimes, playing against my friend's more masculine side—I'm sorry, really."

"Ach, you little bitch," she says and stumbles off her stool, back towards the tables, where the women are dancing.

"Boy," says the bartender, "that one was really potted. You did okay though, kid, I like your style. Gotta remember no one has a right to give you any shit. Huh, left a whole dollar on the counter—well, I'll save it for her if she misses it." I felt a little like a boxer in training. My style. (177)

"But you don't think I kind of hook in too hard with my left?" I ask the woman behind the bar, but she has already lapsed back into her usual laconic state.

I go look for Peggy. The gray-suited woman has seemingly only been to the bathroom and is beginning to reconsider and start looking for me again. Peggy is in the corner making theater talk with some young actress who is not bad looking.

"Peggy," I say, "Peggy, we have to get out of here. That woman—you see, over there—she has a knife, I think, Peggy." I say, "Peggy we have to get the fuck out of here because I just rejected her pass at me and she is not at all happy about it."

"Fuck it. Inez, you'll never learn anything, will

you? Okay, okay. See you later, Kathy, give me a call sometime, will you?"

"Sure," says the girl Peggy was fondling, a little saddened.

"I'll take care of you, my dear," says Peggy, coming back to our own game. "Am I not your gallant escort? Come, dear, let me get your wrap. Let us proceed to make our exit calmly so as not to arouse any trouble or bad feeling." I roll my eyes around in their sockets. It is about three a.m. anyway, an hour before closing, and just as well.

As soon as we get out I sigh, Peggy pokes me in the ribs and I crack up. "Fuck fuck fuck fuck, Inez," says Peggy, "fuck. I am drunk as—as—drunk as what? What as drunk? What as drunk as I? Good thing you are driving otherwise we would be dead. But I never knew how to drive. Anyway. Anyway. Wait. Let us get some coffee before we go back across the bridge. There is a fine little place I know in North Beach—what time is it, anyway?"

"It's after three, Peggy."

"Fuck fuck fuck again. What I mean is, it's closed. How about the Copper Penny in Berkeley? If I don't pass out by then?"

"Okay." We get into the car and drive off across the Bay Bridge. I am not doing so hot myself, being somewhat shook up and a little tipsy, but we manage. In the Copper Penny, Peggy revives and cross-examines me about my adventures with the woman in the gray suit. When I get to the part about taking me to Los Angeles Peggy chokes on her coffee. I know it would have been better if I could have talked about it, with this woman, about how she was trying to impress me with the exact behavior I hate in men, when they do it.

But we are not judging, Peggy and me. It is after all a time of great confusion in the world, it is hard not to get mangled in some way. In general, we approve of the whole evening as a nice chapter in Riverfinger history, and Peggy kisses me every time the waitress walks by, for its shock value.

Back on Blake Street it is four a.m. when we giggle our best not to wake Eulalee and her latest boyfriend. Shutting the door to our cubicle, I undress Peggy who falls all over me in this effort because she is so drunk. When at last we are both naked, I carry her to bed in my arms (which gives me great satisfaction) and she rubs her head over and over again against my breast until we are settled on the mattress, where she takes my nipple in her teeth.

"Ow! You little bitch! Watch out for *my* knife wounds!" I say as she bites me. I laugh. She laughs and we hug each other. Riverfinger women are known for their laughter. I rub my hands in arcs across her rib cage. She is lying there smiling at me, reaching up to tousle my hair.

"Inez, I'm too tired to move."

"That's okay, buddy. Feel like being responsive?"

"I'd love to be."

I am above her, my knees on either side of her body, moving my breasts down along her limbs slowly. The hair of her vagina is blond, she is soft and smooth, there, cool against my forehead as I spread her thighs apart with my chin—rubbing the soft fuzz down one leg and then the other, licking it in circles, coming closer, kneading her stomach gently, like delicate, delicate bread, with my hands, and then my tongue is in between the lips of her vagina. What a taste that is! Salt and sour and sweet all at once—the bathhouse of Coney Island, the cotton candy circus. Sweet Peggy, little Peggy, like a mango I open you with my teeth and push my tongue as far deep as it will go—which is hard work, for a tongue. Slipping tastebuds in and out of the soft lining of her sex. Then I suck on her clitoris as it stiffens and she begins to moan in tune to the sucking motion I make. The wetness is like Cleopatra's milk bath to my face. She wiggles and moans and pulls at my hair.

ooooo Innnnyyyy Innnnnnnyyyyyyy ah oooo and similar exclamations. I am filled with my happiness, I am next to my desire, nothing on earth could taste better than this, but it is late now, and I'm tired.

(180)

I come up for air, wearing her wetness on my jaw like the beard of a Roman victor, out battling wild men in Abysinia for six months and then home in the chariot to the roar of crowds. The new Amazon warrior priestess.

She pushes my head into her belly where I wipe my face, laughing, ready to sleep myself, our asses grazing on the nocturnal pastures of each other, after a long day in the new city of gold.

The next day Eulalee came back from her morning dance classes to find us still in bed.

"Inez? Peggy?" Groan. Moan. What time is it? One-thirty. Was I having a dream, what was it? Pull the sheets up, christ. Come in Eulalee.

Eulalee sat on the bed edge with the mail, which contained an aereogramme from Israel.

"This," she said, "is strangely enough a letter from Abby to me."

Front and center, everyone. "Abby, Abby? Abby! Jesus christ—what does she say???!!"

"Here, read it."

July 25, '71

Dear Eulalee,

I'm sorry to bother you after all these years but I haven't been able it seems to reach Inez or Peggy. (181) Do you know where either of them are? I am leaving Israel August 22 for Amsterdam, spending a couple days there, then flying to my parents' house in N.Y. I'm sure neither of them would want to hang around there but maybe we could meet in Massachusetts, or something. My father was here a couple months ago and I found out that I have some kind of inheritance coming out of my grandmother which I can't understand but it is 20 thousand or something equally absurd and I am thinking about buying land in Canada. I don't know what else to say, as this is a letter to you and not to them and I haven't seen you for three years. It is nice in Jerusalem./ I am sitting here eating a salad. You should see the size of radishes in this country, they're like oranges. And oranges here are absolutely fantastic, especially when you go for long hikes in the desert—took one for five hours and discovered two springs with a fantastic pool—perfect for swimming—cold and deep. All kinds of incredible wildflowers—beautiful things to behold. It is really like a Portland summer day today, so nice . . .

I guess I am just filling up this so as not to waste paper. I would like very much for there to be a meeting between me and Inez that is not full of bitterness or hassling, and I think that time has begun, we shall see. It will have to be a new thing, if we both want it to be again, and I for one am not making any promises, but—anyway if you know where she is, tell her I'll be at my parents' house on Long Island after August 30, and she should call there—

> thank you muchly Eulalee
> much love, Shalom, Abby

(182)

Now I remember what I was dreaming before Eulalee woke us up. I dreamed I was in a room crowded with strangers. Suddenly a figure, a little like Alice in Wonderland, eyes closed, crying, arms outstretched, walked towards me, through the crowd. Everyone was silent. Everyone knew that this was the dead girl, the child we all had murdered. No one will touch her, they turn their backs. I shiver in my sleep, but then pick her up. She is stiff in my arms, but her hands clasp me, and they're warm. I am amazed that I have acted with such kindness and affection. I hold her and I say, "When we meet again, I'll take care of you. This time I promise." She opens her eyes and smiles at me. First her face is the face of Rainbo Woman, then it is my face. She rises smiling, levitates on her back above all of us, and disappears floating through a wall.

"Hey Inez, what're you thinking about?" Peggy starts to tickle her, and she opens her eyes. Eulalee holds her hand.

"I'm thinking," Inez said, "about the happy ending to the pornographic novel of our lives."

Afterword—20 years go by

I was 21 when I wrote *Riverfinger Women* in 1971. *Riverfinger* was among the first of the second wave's lesbian novels, the first to have Jewish protagonists, and it came directly from my stubborn wilfulness not to be a tragic queer. My determination to love my scary lesbian life, no matter what. When June Arnold and Parke Bowman, the founders of Daughters, Inc., published it in 1974, they changed my life—or more accurately, pushed me along a path I meant to go. Barbara Grier has reprinted it here as it was first published. I reread it, expecting to be embarrassed by my swaggering, politically naive, humanist younger self—and wasn't disappointed. But I was amused and pleased as well.

Context helps. Books have a life of their own *(185)* in the world after we write them. They go out and do all kinds of things in our names, most of which we never know.* Still, I want to place *Riverfinger* in its time, and I want to tell the story of its relationship to Daughters, Inc.

In my last year at college, one of my teachers suggested I write a book. He knew the publisher who'd first printed Henry Miller in the States. This publisher was planning a new series of literary soft-core pornographic romance novels aimed at liberal straight women titillated by the "sexual

---

*I met a lesbian once in Osento (the women's bath house in San Francisco) who told me after she read *Riverfinger,* she dropped out of college and started travelling the country by jumping freight trains.

revolution." My teacher obliquely suggested a lesbian novel might do well in this series.

I have been a lesbian all my life: I knew I loved womyn when I fell in love with my nursery school bus driver, and I knew the word as soon as my first psychiatrist told me I wasn't a homosexual when I was 12. By the time I was 21 I had read a fair sample of lesbian pornography written by men. *Dykes on Bikes,* for instance, was passed around my high school—in it a bored society lady invites a depraved lesbian cycle gang to rape her twin daughters so they'll be primed for sex with her. I'd read a few quasi-psychological studies which described lesbians as wearing men's clothes and smoking cigars—the ultimate in incomprehensible depravity. I'd seen and/or read *The Children's Hour, The Killing of Sister George* and *The Fox,* where the lesbians all get killed (one way or another) in the end. I'd read about the *Well of Loneliness,* but *Nightwood,* by Djuna Barnes, was the only lesbian novel written by a lesbian that I'd read. The morbid angst of Barnes' lesbians suited my adolescent understanding that a lesbian's prospects were, at best, bleak. I carried *Nightwood* under my arm the entire year I was 16, and later hung out in front of Djuna Barnes' apartment house on Patchen Place in New York, hoping to get a glimpse of the recluse. I treasure the postcard she wrote me giving permission to use the quote that's the epigram for *Riverfinger.* Her lesbians can hardly be considered role models, but her love of language, her ability to clothe her characters' complexity and despair in words, her ability to get those words printed, were a revelation to me.

* * * * *

In 1969 Inez and Abby Riverfingers knew there must be other queers in Chicago, but there was no place to look for them since they were too young to go to bars (even if they could have figured out how to find one). They felt like the only ones. In 1971 there was no Naiad Press, no Daughters, Inc., no Firebrand, no Kitchen Table: Women of Color Press, no Aunt Lute Foundation, no *Nice Jewish Girls–a Jewish Lesbian Anthology,* no *This Bridge Called My Back–writing by Radical Women of Color,* no magazines except the Ladder (which I had never seen) and the first women's liberation manifestos that were appearing in underground papers. But a tremendous excitement was building. Consciousness-raising groups were everywhere.

My senior year in college, I started a Gay Liberation group with a boy I knew, only to find myself making coffee for faggots. The lesbians wouldn't come near Gay Liberation. I went to a Women's Liberation meeting and found straight women talking about their lives with men. Where were the lesbians? They didn't want to hang around with a dyke who wore a Gay Liberation button everywhere, that's for sure. I was lonely and isolated.

(187)

So when my teacher suggested I write a novel, it seemed like a good idea. I could write a "pornographic" "hip" lesbian novel with a happy ending. It would be a first, it would be right on time, sell a million copies, and I wouldn't have to worry anymore about what I was going to do for a living when I got out of college.

Inez makes a big deal out of writing a pornographic novel, and although she explains what she means pretty well, her understanding of "pornography" was limited. At the time, while I understood that pornography was the vehicle for men's objectification of women, I also harbored the beliefs that every expression of human sexuality was a sacred part of the life force, that violence done to women was an individual and aberrant act (as opposed to a global war from which every man draws power), and that women who objected to all pornography (not "just" snuff films) were repressed prudes.* At the time, I thought a lesbian writing about lesbian sex and emotional life fell into the same "outlaw" camp as men writing for *Penthouse,* making us all rebels together against the "establishment." I didn't get it that *Penthouse* is a stone's throw from the White House.

(188)

Because I had set out to satisfy the category of "hip pornography," which was all I could see as available to me in 1971, I thought I had to include at least some hetero- and bi-sexual scenes. There was (and is) an enormous pressure on lesbians to not be "exclusive," and many quasi-

---

*While I don't think this now, I have many reservations about the anti-porn movement, which revolve around the issues of priorities and legislative reform. I can't see how what the state does around this issue will ever be in womyn's best interests until womyn control the state. On the other hand, I take heart every time I read about dykes pouring buckets of blood in porno shops—and I don't read about it often enough.

anthropological arguments about how, in a different world, we'd all be bi-sexual. There wasn't so much as a women's bookstore in New York, Portland, Chicago, San Francisco or Los Angeles when the events in *Riverfinger* took place. I submitted, and I mean that literally, to my friends' arguments about the naturalness of bi-sexuality, to the idea that there was something of value to lesbians in reading about any form of heterosexual or male gay sex. We have never lived in that "different world" free of all institutions of oppression, and will not see it in our lifetimes. In retrospect, I experience the intense pressure put on me (by straight women and both gay and straight men) to define myself as "at least" bi-sexual as a form of violent coercion. The world we *do* live in hates and fears lesbians for very political reasons, especially lesbians who claim the right to live their lives for and with other lesbians. That hasn't changed in the last twenty years.

(189)

But back in early 1971, I put a plank across the arms of an old easy chair, popped an amphetamine,* and wrote the first third of *Riverfinger Women* in 18 hours flat.

Gay Liberation had attracted a few womyn

Riverfinger reflects two very different drug cultures: the "tune in, turn on, drop out" movement of the '60s, and lesbian bar culture. While I take exception to much of the 12-Step ideology, I am proud of the new sobriety and moderation of my lesbian community. It amazes me sometimes how many of us have managed to survive and flourish.

who'd come for a meeting and then leave. One of these, a tuba player who confessed, during our somewhat desultory one-night stand, that what she really wanted to be was a faggot, turned me on to an arts community in Western Massachusetts. After college graduation (the last time I wore a dress, the only time I heard Anaïs Nin speak) I went to the arts community and finished the manuscript.

I brought the book to the New York publisher and waited. While I was waiting, I crashed my Travelall Van on a dirt road, and ended up staying in Western Massachusetts, where I found the Valley Women's Center in Northampton. After about a year, the publisher sent my book back, saying it wasn't really what they were looking for at all. I got more involved in the women's center, started distributing women's films, lived on welfare and moved into a women's collective where I was the only lesbian. My manuscript got rejected by Knopf. I put it in the closet. Then an ex-lover (from the arts community) who'd gone to school with one of June Arnold's daughters sent me a flyer about this new women's press, Daughters, Inc.

Daughters accepted *Riverfinger* for their second group of books, to come out in 1974, with the provision that I rewrite it. I drove up to Vermont to meet these womyn. They were white dykes in their late forties or early fifties then, hard-drinking, arrogant, charming, inspiring and inspired. Their books would never go out of print, they would treat their authors with respect, their contracts were a mere formality, we would always be able to work out anything, feminist to feminist. I loved them.

I remember coming back from Vermont feeling like a "comer"—lesbians had reached out to me and said: pick it up you can do it make us proud. This is something that happens to lesbians with a frequency like winning the lottery. It's not very often that as you come into the beginning of your adult life other womyn welcome you and appreciate what you come with, encourage you to do your work, help you to the best of their ability.* At the time I felt they saw in me the new generation of their hope, although June insisted she would never trust anyone under forty.

The summer of 1973 I rewrote for two months and sent it back. June cut out a third of the rewrite and sent it to the printers without telling me. She was a gifted editor, I overwrote (shuttling between my ideas about literature, hip and feminism), and she apologized profusely. Although I haven't looked at the original manuscript in at least fifteen years, I think she did me a great favor—but she still should have told me first. *(191)*

While *Riverfinger* was in production, Daughters came out with their first list, which included *The Cook and The Carpenter, Nerves, Early Losses, The Treasure* and *Rubyfruit Jungle.* I was invited to the celebration. I could bring my friends. Four of us left Western Massachusetts in our best city clothes.

In addition to the farmhouse in Vermont, June

---

*Unlike the lottery, we have the power to increase the odds. I want lesbian communities where every single lesbian is a comer.

owned a townhouse in the Village (the bottom floor was the NY Women's Coffeehouse for years). While she and Parke were dedicated to the women's movement, they wanted to launch a "real" publishing house on the big boys' turf. They were fighting on two fronts at once: struggling to actually create a lesbian and feminist audience, and to prove to the straight publishing world that they could succeed. I thought they were rich—they were rich compared to everyone else I knew. I had no idea how undercapitalized they were for what they wanted to accomplish. For the party, they filled a refrigerator with champagne, hired a women's band, invited everyone. By the time we got there, late in the afternoon, the last of the male press was leaving. Our "best city clothes" were overshadowed in an instant by dykes in tuxedos and boas, Rita Mae striding around in flashy cowboy boots. "Everyone" was there. We tried not to be impressed. We drank all the champagne we could hold and danced. We were young and at the center of a revolution that knew how to party.

All my life I wanted to be a published writer. I had been an outsider everywhere I went since I was a child for six different reasons. But by the time *Riverfinger* came out, I was experiencing being an insider for the first time—of belonging with a group of womyn and working for ideals we shared. I was scrutinizing the class and skin privilege that gave me both the material for and the freedom to write *Riverfinger*. I didn't want "being published" to set me apart from the lesbians (or even the straight women) I worked with in the women's center. It was dawning on me that writers could be a working part of their communities, not isolated by either their "stance" or their accomplishments. It took me awhile to learn that not wanting to get caught up in "fame and fortune" (such as it is among lesbians) was no reason not to be proud of what you create. The first time I met Linda Shear,* in a discussion of the "CLIT papers," I told her it was no big deal that I had published *Riverfinger Women*. "Wait a second," she said, "you mean to tell me you are one of maybe five lesbians in the world who has been able to publish a lesbian novel with a lesbian publishing house, and it's no big deal? What's wrong with you?"

Caught up in my self-doubt and the intensity of political debate around me, I went into high gear. I was struggling with the ideologies and practicalities of both socialist-feminism and lesbian separatism. In 1974–75 I co-founded Lesbian Gardens (a lesbian space above the women's center which had a coffeehouse, small bookstore and housed our local dyke patrol), co-produced a women's film festival, was one of the organizers of the Connecticut Valley Bi-Millennial Lesbian Celebration, did grand jury work and was on the organizing committee for the 1975 Socialist-Feminist Conference in Yellow Springs. By the time the Socialist-Feminist Conference was

---

*Linda was the founder of Family of Woman band, which was based in Chicago in the early '70s. Her only album, *Linda Shear: A Lesbian Portrait*, is a wonderful, not-to-be-missed piece of lesbian cultural herstory.

over, I believed that both socialism and feminism were male-defined ideologies, that their purpose was to change the appearance of the state so that it looked like everyone was getting a fairer shake, while the same white boys kept control.

I went to Vermont and rented an apartment for the summer, with the royalties I got from *Riverfinger,** five miles from June and Parke's farmhouse. During the day I tried to write a novel about the women's collective I'd lived in for two years; at night I'd have a beer or two and write whatever I felt like writing—which turned out to be the short stories that became *They Will Know Me By My Teeth*. Sometimes I'd go over to the farmhouse and join the dinnertime arguments about writing, love, class, ageism, separatism, racism, the Sagaris Institute.**

It's hard to explain how much I loved June and Parke—of course some of it was because they encouraged me. But the other part was about how much they wanted to encourage a women's revolution—how they had a vision where there would be room for every woman to speak for herself, at last. How they used their resources to help create a world where it would be possible for lesbians and women to survive.

---

*This was approximately $1,500 at the time. While *Riverfinger* was in print, I made a little more than $3,000 from it. In case you were wondering.

**It seems so far away now, and all I really remember about Sagaris is driving there with June, Samn Stockwell and a couple other lesbians, to try and get them not to take Playboy money. Sagaris was intended as a model for a new, non-hierarchical feminist learning center.

In the next three years, after I went back to my life in Northampton, we fought almost every time we talked. I changed my name,* didn't want to publish anything anywhere a man might gain access. I was angry, defensive, and in the midst of the dyke wars.** Once June invited me to go along on a speaking engagement she had at Hampshire College. There she called *Riverfinger* a feminist novel. I said it may be a feminist novel, but I was only a feminist during the brief period in which I rewrote it. She never invited me again.

They moved to Houston. *Riverfinger* went out of print, and it seemed like Daughters had closed. When I was moving across country in 1979, we had dinner together in Houston. They were drunk and belligerent. June said, "You've forgotten women are complex." I don't remember whether I was polite or inflammatory.

In 1980, while spending a night in Eugene, Thyme Seagull mentioned she'd just got a copy of the new book we were both in. "What book?" "*The Woman Who Lost Her Names,*" she said, which turned out to be an anthology of Jewish women's writings published by Harper & Row, in which an

(195)

---

*Okay, so I changed my name. If you want to know why, read the essay "The Expatriot and Her Name" in *In Versions–writing by dykes, queers and lesbians,* edited by Betsy Warland, Press Gang Books, 1991.

**"The dyke wars" were a series of political battles around separatism, class and race that were fought on an extremely personal level almost everywhere there was an active lesbian and women's movement in the mid-70s–early 80s. Everyone got hurt. I still consider myself a lesbian separatist/radical, and my current understanding of separatism allows me a lot more room to engage with other lesbians than it did in 1977.

excerpt from *Riverfinger* appeared. I was shocked. How could June and Parke decide for me when and how I wanted to portray my understanding of being a Jew? Didn't they know I didn't want to publish with men's publishing houses? Hadn't June promised to never again do anything with my writing without my knowledge? What happened to "don't worry about the contract—we'll work everything out feminist to feminist?" I wrote them outraged letters they didn't answer. Then someone told me that June had brain cancer.

They must have known I would hate what they'd done even if the contract we'd signed in '73 gave them the legal right. I figured they never wrote back because of June's sickness, but I wish I knew what made them do it. I was furious about the excerpt and furious with the frustration and grief of knowing I'd never get the chance to work it out with June.

(196)

A lesbian lawyer agreed to have the next letters go out on her letterhead. I got a brief note from Parke giving the rights back to me. I wrote June a letter, saying I didn't want her to go without knowing I thought she was a class A bitch, that I was glad for our relationship, and I loved her tremendously. June died in 1982.

In 1990, Bonnie Zimmerman published a wonderful volume of lesbian literary criticism, *The Safe Sea of Women* (the title a quote from June's *The Cook and The Carpenter*). Bonnie gave a lot of thought and credit to the early Daughters' books, which inspired Barbara Grier to call me with Naiad's offer to reprint *Riverfinger*. "Not without an introduction," I said.

"Nobody reads Introductions," Barbara replied, "Would you settle for an Afterword?" "Done," I said, and it is.

Okay, so you still want to know what happened to the Riverfingers. Peggy Warren became a computer analyst and went into a recovery program. About five years ago I heard she came out, but I haven't heard anything about her since. Abby Riverfingers became a carpenter and then an architect, used part of her inheritance to help establish a lesbian foundation. She and Inez remain good friends. Inez Riverfingers, if she ever had that dope money, doesn't have it now. She's living happily ever after, anyway.

UNDER THE SOUTHERN CROSS by Claire McNab. 192 pp.
Romantic nights Down Under. ISBN 1-56280-011-6 $9.95

RIVERFINGER WOMEN by Elana Nachman/Dykewomon.
208 pp. Classic Lesbian/feminist novel. ISBN 1-56280-013-2 8.95

A CERTAIN DISCONTENT by Cleve Boutell. 240 pp. A unique
coterie of women. ISBN 1-56280-009-4 9.95

GRASSY FLATS by Penny Hayes. 256 pp. Lesbian romance in
the '30s. ISBN 1-56280-010-8 9.95

A SINGULAR SPY by Amanda K. Williams. 192 pp. 3rd spy novel
featuring Lesbian agent Madison McGuire. ISBN 1-56280-008-6 8.95

THE END OF APRIL by Penny Sumner. 240 pp. A Victoria Cross
Mystery. First in a series. ISBN 1-56280-007-8 8.95

A FLIGHT OF ANGELS by Sarah Aldridge. 240 pp. Romance set at
the National Gallery of Art ISBN 1-56280-001-9 9.95

HOUSTON TOWN by Deborah Powell. 208 pp. A Hollis Carpenter
mystery. Second in a series. ISBN 1-56280-006-X 8.95

KISS AND TELL by Robbi Sommers. 192 pp. Scorching stories by
the author of *Pleasures*. ISBN 1-56280-005-1 8.95

STILL WATERS by Pat Welch. 208 pp. Second in the Helen
Black mystery series. ISBN 0-941483-97-5 8.95

MURDER IS GERMANE by Karen Saum. 224 pp. The 2nd
Brigid Donovan mystery. ISBN 0-941483-98-3 8.95

TO LOVE AGAIN by Evelyn Kennedy. 208 pp. Wildly
romantic love story. ISBN 0-941483-85-1 9.95

IN THE GAME by Nikki Baker. 192 pp. A Virginia Kelly
mystery. First in a series. ISBN 01-56280-004-3 8.95

AVALON by Mary Jane Jones. 256 pp. A Lesbian Arthurian
romance. ISBN 0-941483-96-7 9.95

STRANDED by Camarin Grae. 320 pp. Entertaining, riveting
adventure. ISBN 0-941483-99-1 9.95

THE DAUGHTERS OF ARTEMIS by Lauren Wright Douglas.
240 pp. Third Caitlin Reece mystery. ISBN 0-941483-95-9 8.95

CLEARWATER by Catherine Ennis. 176 pp. Romantic secrets
of a small Louisiana town. ISBN 0-941483-65-7 8.95

THE HALLELUJAH MURDERS by Dorothy Tell. 176 pp.
Second Poppy Dillworth mystery. ISBN 0-941483-88-6   8.95

ZETA BASE by Judith Alguire. 208 pp. Lesbian triangle
on a future Earth. ISBN 0-941483-94-0   9.95

SECOND CHANCE by Jackie Calhoun. 256 pp. Contemporary
Lesbian lives and loves. ISBN 0-941483-93-2   9.95

MURDER BY TRADITION by Katherine V. Forrest. 288 pp.
A Kate Delafield Mystery. 4th in a series. ISBN 0-941483-89-4   18.95

BENEDICTION by Diane Salvatore. 272 pp. Striking,
contemporary romantic novel. ISBN 0-941483-90-8   9.95

CALLING RAIN by Karen Marie Christa Minns. 240 pp.
Spellbinding, erotic love story ISBN 0-941483-87-8   9.95

BLACK IRIS by Jeane Harris. 192 pp. Caroline's hidden past . . .
ISBN 0-941483-68-1   8.95

TOUCHWOOD by Karin Kallmaker. 240 pp. Loving, May/
December romance. ISBN 0-941483-76-2   8.95

BAYOU CITY SECRETS by Deborah Powell. 224 pp. A Hollis
Carpenter mystery. First in a series. ISBN 0-941483-91-6   8.95

COP OUT by Claire McNab. 208 pp. 4th Det. Insp. Carol Ashton
mystery. ISBN 0-941483-84-3   8.95

LODESTAR by Phyllis Horn. 224 pp. Romantic, fast-moving
adventure. ISBN 0-941483-83-5   8.95

THE BEVERLY MALIBU by Katherine V. Forrest. 288 pp. A
Kate Delafield Mystery. 3rd in a series. (HC)   ISBN 0-941483-47-9   16.95
Paperback   ISBN 0-941483-48-7   9.95

THAT OLD STUDEBAKER by Lee Lynch. 272 pp. Andy's affair
with Regina and her attachment to her beloved car.
ISBN 0-941483-82-7   9.95

PASSION'S LEGACY by Lori Paige. 224 pp. Sarah is swept into
the arms of Augusta Pym in this delightful historical romance.
ISBN 0-941483-81-9   8.95

THE PROVIDENCE FILE by Amanda Kyle Williams. 256 pp.
Second espionage thriller featuring lesbian agent Madison McGuire
ISBN 0-941483-92-4   8.95

I LEFT MY HEART by Jaye Maiman. 320 pp. A Robin Miller
Mystery. First in a series. ISBN 0-941483-72-X   9.95

THE PRICE OF SALT by Patricia Highsmith (writing as Claire
Morgan). 288 pp. Classic lesbian novel, first issued in 1952 . . .
acknowledged by its author under her own, very famous, name.
ISBN 1-56280-003-5   8.95

SIDE BY SIDE by Isabel Miller. 256 pp. From beloved author of
Patience and Sarah. ISBN 0-941483-77-0   8.95

SOUTHBOUND by Sheila Ortiz Taylor. 240 pp. Hilarious sequel
to *Faultline*.   ISBN 0-941483-78-9   8.95

STAYING POWER: LONG TERM LESBIAN COUPLES
by Susan E. Johnson. 352 pp. Joys of coupledom.
                                                    ISBN 0-941-483-75-4   12.95

SLICK by Camarin Grae. 304 pp. Exotic, erotic adventure.
                                                    ISBN 0-941483-74-6   9.95

NINTH LIFE by Lauren Wright Douglas. 256 pp. A Caitlin
Reece mystery. 2nd in a series.   ISBN 0-941483-50-9   8.95

PLAYERS by Robbi Sommers. 192 pp. Sizzling, erotic novel.
                                                    ISBN 0-941483-73-8   8.95

MURDER AT RED ROOK RANCH by Dorothy Tell. 224 pp.
First Poppy Dillworth adventure.   ISBN 0-941483-80-0   8.95

LESBIAN SURVIVAL MANUAL by Rhonda Dicksion.
112 pp. Cartoons!   ISBN 0-941483-71-1   8.95

A ROOM FULL OF WOMEN by Elisabeth Nonas. 256 pp.
Contemporary Lesbian lives.   ISBN 0-941483-69-X   8.95

MURDER IS RELATIVE by Karen Saum. 256 pp. The first
Brigid Donovan mystery.   ISBN 0-941483-70-3   8.95

PRIORITIES by Lynda Lyons 288 pp. Science fiction with
a twist.   ISBN 0-941483-66-5   8.95

THEME FOR DIVERSE INSTRUMENTS by Jane Rule. 208
pp. Powerful romantic lesbian stories.   ISBN 0-941483-63-0   8.95

LESBIAN QUERIES by Hertz & Ertman. 112 pp. The questions
you were too embarrassed to ask.   ISBN 0-941483-67-3   8.95

CLUB 12 by Amanda Kyle Williams. 288 pp. Espionage thriller
featuring a lesbian agent!   ISBN 0-941483-64-9   8.95

DEATH DOWN UNDER by Claire McNab. 240 pp. 3rd Det.
Insp. Carol Ashton mystery.   ISBN 0-941483-39-8   8.95

MONTANA FEATHERS by Penny Hayes. 256 pp. Vivian and
Elizabeth find love in frontier Montana.   ISBN 0-941483-61-4   8.95

CHESAPEAKE PROJECT by Phyllis Horn. 304 pp. Jessie &
Meredith in perilous adventure.   ISBN 0-941483-58-4   8.95

LIFESTYLES by Jackie Calhoun. 224 pp. Contemporary Lesbian
lives and loves.   ISBN 0-941483-57-6   8.95

VIRAGO by Karen Marie Christa Minns. 208 pp. Darsen has
chosen Ginny.   ISBN 0-941483-56-8   8.95

WILDERNESS TREK by Dorothy Tell. 192 pp. Six women on
vacation learning "new" skills.   ISBN 0-941483-60-6   8.95

MURDER BY THE BOOK by Pat Welch. 256 pp. A Helen
Black Mystery. First in a series.   ISBN 0-941483-59-2   8.95

BERRIGAN by Vicki P. McConnell. 176 pp. Youthful Lesbian —
romantic, idealistic Berrigan.   ISBN 0-941483-55-X   8.95

LESBIANS IN GERMANY by Lillian Faderman & B. Eriksson.
128 pp. Fiction, poetry, essays.   ISBN 0-941483-62-2   8.95

THERE'S SOMETHING I'VE BEEN MEANING TO TELL
YOU Ed. by Loralee MacPike. 288 pp. Gay men and lesbians
coming out to their children.   ISBN 0-941483-44-4   9.95
                                              ISBN 0-941483-54-1   16.95

LIFTING BELLY by Gertrude Stein. Ed. by Rebecca Mark. 104
pp. Erotic poetry.   ISBN 0-941483-51-7   8.95
                                              ISBN 0-941483-53-3   14.95

ROSE PENSKI by Roz Perry. 192 pp. Adult lovers in a long-term
relationship.   ISBN 0-941483-37-1   8.95

AFTER THE FIRE by Jane Rule. 256 pp. Warm, human novel
by this incomparable author.   ISBN 0-941483-45-2   8.95

SUE SLATE, PRIVATE EYE by Lee Lynch. 176 pp. The gay
folk of Peacock Alley are *all cats*.   ISBN 0-941483-52-5   8.95

CHRIS by Randy Salem. 224 pp. Golden oldie. Handsome Chris
and her adventures.   ISBN 0-941483-42-8   8.95

THREE WOMEN by March Hastings. 232 pp. Golden oldie. A
triangle among wealthy sophisticates.   ISBN 0-941483-43-6   8.95

RICE AND BEANS by Valeria Taylor. 232 pp. Love and
romance on poverty row.   ISBN 0-941483-41-X   8.95

PLEASURES by Robbi Sommers. 204 pp. Unprecedented
eroticism.   ISBN 0-941483-49-5   8.95

EDGEWISE by Camarin Grae. 372 pp. Spellbinding
adventure.   ISBN 0-941483-19-3   9.95

FATAL REUNION by Claire McNab. 224 pp. 2nd Det. Inspec.
Carol Ashton mystery.   ISBN 0-941483-40-1   8.95

KEEP TO ME STRANGER by Sarah Aldridge. 372 pp. Romance
set in a department store dynasty.   ISBN 0-941483-38-X   9.95

HEARTSCAPE by Sue Gambill. 204 pp. American lesbian in
Portugal.   ISBN 0-941483-33-9   8.95

IN THE BLOOD by Lauren Wright Douglas. 252 pp. Lesbian
science fiction adventure fantasy   ISBN 0-941483-22-3   8.95

THE BEE'S KISS by Shirley Verel. 216 pp. Delicate, delicious
romance.   ISBN 0-941483-36-3   8.95

RAGING MOTHER MOUNTAIN by Pat Emmerson. 264 pp.
Furosa Firechild's adventures in Wonderland. ISBN 0-941483-35-5   8.95

IN EVERY PORT by Karin Kallmaker. 228 pp. Jessica's sexy,
adventuresome travels.   ISBN 0-941483-37-7   8.95

OF LOVE AND GLORY by Evelyn Kennedy. 192 pp. Exciting
WWII romance.   ISBN 0-941483-32-0   8.95

CLICKING STONES by Nancy Tyler Glenn. 288 pp. Love
transcending time.   ISBN 0-941483-31-2   9.95

SURVIVING SISTERS by Gail Pass. 252 pp. Powerful love
story.   ISBN 0-941483-16-9   8.95

SOUTH OF THE LINE by Catherine Ennis. 216 pp. Civil War
adventure.   ISBN 0-941483-29-0   8.95

WOMAN PLUS WOMAN by Dolores Klaich. 300 pp. Supurb
Lesbian overview.   ISBN 0-941483-28-2   9.95

SLOW DANCING AT MISS POLLY'S by Sheila Ortiz Taylor.
96 pp. Lesbian Poetry   ISBN 0-941483-30-4   7.95

DOUBLE DAUGHTER by Vicki P. McConnell. 216 pp. A Nyla
Wade Mystery, third in the series.   ISBN 0-941483-26-6   8.95

HEAVY GILT by Delores Klaich. 192 pp. Lesbian detective/
disappearing homophobes/upper class gay society.

                                       ISBN 0-941483-25-8   8.95

THE FINER GRAIN by Denise Ohio. 216 pp. Brilliant young
college lesbian novel.   ISBN 0-941483-11-8   8.95

THE AMAZON TRAIL by Lee Lynch. 216 pp. Life, travel & lore
of famous lesbian author.   ISBN 0-941483-27-4   8.95

HIGH CONTRAST by Jessie Lattimore. 264 pp. Women of the
Crystal Palace.   ISBN 0-941483-17-7   8.95

OCTOBER OBSESSION by Meredith More. Josie's rich, secret
Lesbian life.   ISBN 0-941483-18-5   8.95

LESBIAN CROSSROADS by Ruth Baetz. 276 pp. Contemporary
Lesbian lives.   ISBN 0-941483-21-5   9.95

BEFORE STONEWALL: THE MAKING OF A GAY AND
LESBIAN COMMUNITY by Andrea Weiss & Greta Schiller.
96 pp., 25 illus.   ISBN 0-941483-20-7   7.95

WE WALK THE BACK OF THE TIGER by Patricia A. Murphy.
192 pp. Romantic Lesbian novel/beginning women's movement.
                                       ISBN 0-941483-13-4   8.95

SUNDAY'S CHILD by Joyce Bright. 216 pp. Lesbian athletics, at
last the novel about sports.   ISBN 0-941483-12-6   8.95

These are just a few of the many Naiad Press titles — we are the oldest and
largest lesbian/feminist publishing company in the world. Please request a
complete catalog. We offer personal service; we encourage and welcome direct
mail orders from individuals who have limited access to bookstores carrying
our publications.